Satan's Lamp

William Jackson is a British author of gay horror fiction. His characters inhabit a homonormative world in stark contrast to the heteronormativity of so much horror narrative. His writing looks at oppression, the inherent seductiveness of evil and the corruption, or moral decay, often masked by beauty. He cites his influences as Richard Laymon, Dennis Wheatley and Fred Mustard Stewart.

Jackson is a master at reaching to the heart of the reader's deepest fears - then deftly twisting his pen. His fiction has been described as *Hammer horror for the 21st Century*.

www.williamjackson.uk

By the same author:

SHORT STORIES:

Shapes in the Dark
A Collection of 18 Short Stories

Kill Johnny
Limited Edition

The Brutal Kiss
Limited Edition

NON FICTION
as Moon Laramie:

The Zombie Inside

Spirit of Garbo

Theosophy & the Search for Happiness
with Annie Besant

Blavatsky Unveiled:
The Writings of H. P. Blavatsky in Modern English
Volume One

WILLIAM JACKSON
SATAN'S LAMP

INTRODUCED BY LINDA HAYDEN

William Jackson (signature)

martin firrell company

First published in 2023 by Martin Firrell Company Ltd. Unit 4 City Limits, Danehill, Reading RG6 4UP, UK.

ISBN 978-1-912622-39-9

Text is set in Caslon 11pt on 13pt.

for my husband

thanks

I would like to thank the following people for their help and advice: Ian Hogarth from the Association of Lighthouse Keepers for aiding me in my search for an advisory keeper; David Appleby, ex-lighthouse keeper, for advising me on pertinent aspects of the service; Geoff Turner and Patrick Tubby from Happisburgh Lighthouse for arranging my visit and Patrick, in particular, for my tour of the station; Pat Boles for her help and advice on trauma; Ian Vinnicombe from the National Coastwatch Institution for pointing me in the right direction when researching air-sea rescue procedures and ops out of Gwennap Head; Hamish Young from HM Coastguard for his help on rescue procedures; Michael Fish and the BBC for permission to reproduce Michael's words from the BBC Weather report on 15th October 1987; and to Linda Hayden for her generous and thoughtful introduction to this volume.

introduction by linda hayden

i

In *The Blood on Satan's Claw* (Tigon, 1971) the inhabitants of a small village are terrorised by an unknown presence. The film's director, Piers Haggard, created an extraordinary atmosphere of wild, frenzied hysteria. I played Angel Blake, a conniving young village girl who convinces the village's youngsters to engage in pagan rituals. They pay homage to the Devil and that ultimately leads to their demise.

A similar wild, frenzied hysteria characterises the drama that unfolds in *Satan's Lamp*. The narrative is a toxic mix of blind panic, human weakness, and sheer terror in the face of the unrelenting hostility of the elements. Just as it did in *The Blood on Satan's Claw*, the presence of something unknown - sly and menacing - gives rise to the raw fear that powers *Satan's Lamp* to its breathtaking conclusion.

ii

When I was just fifteen, I was lucky enough to land the plum role of Lucy in the film *Baby Love* (Avton Film, 1969). From the start, the movie was controversial; its famous tagline, dreamt up by the publicity people, was 'she was old enough to make it but not old enough to see it'.

Flown to New York to publicise the movie, I was transfixed to see myself on an eighty-foot-high poster in Times Square. It was my face, but with huge painted lashes reaching right down over my cheeks. The advertising people had exaggerated the makeup to grotesque proportions, making me look like an evil creature and sending all the wrong messages about the film.

But in an odd twist of fate, this billboard turned out to be an augur of my future with the horror genre - my next film was for Hammer horror - *Taste the Blood of Dracula* (1970) followed closely by *The Blood on Satan's Claw*.

iii

People often behave in ways they never thought possible when they're unable to control the circumstances around them. In *Satan's Lamp*, Norton - the drowned man/possessed entity - is out of control; beyond control; determined to take everyone on Devil's Rock lighthouse down to hell. The novel's protagonist - young Jabe - has somehow to find the determination - the grit - and the means, to fight off the demonic creature that has hijacked

Norton's wrecked body.

It seems the human soul has always craved the jolting excitement of shock, of terror. Not everyone enjoys this kind of experience, of course (and some people will go to almost any lengths to avoid it) but we are all slaves to our emotions in some form or other, whether we care to admit it or not .

The relentless pitch of the battle between good and evil in *Satan's Lamp* takes its inevitable toll. The body count adds up, as it should in any example of the genre worth its salt. But there is also light in the darkness; Jabe finds an unlikely ally and source of strength in ship's cook Brenda, shipwrecked when the lamp on Devil's Rock fails.

An unlikely but complementary pair, Jabe and Brenda must summon all their resources of inner strength to rid the mundane world of the other-worldly monstrosity stalking Devil's Rock; and their success - or otherwise - will shape the future for them both.

iv

The hypocrisy of the Victorian age underscores the story of young Alice Hargood in *Taste the Blood of Dracula*. Alice is seen climbing out of her bedroom window for a tryst with her young man. Her father catches her and takes the whip to her, not uncommon in the draconian morality of the day. Ironically, the next time we see her father, he is in a brothel with several male friends enjoying the professional and lurid attentions of prostitutes. Clearly he is not entirely the strait-laced Victorian gentleman he professes to be. Fear of her tyrannical father and the restrictions placed on young, well-bred girls of this era

11

make Alice extremely vulnerable; the perfect fodder for Count Dracula, lurking patiently in the bushes.

Inevitably, hypocrisy is still out there; it operates now as it always has done, though it is challenged more often than ever before these days.

One of the lighthouse keepers on Devil's Rock is a latent bisexual. Alan Blake can't shake off what he regards as society's prohibitions or his responsibilities as a married father of two boys. No matter how unhappy and unfulfilled his conventional existence has made him, he is simply too afraid to reveal his true nature.

When Alan and Jabe share a moment of fleeting intimacy, hypocrisy inevitably colours the situation, and that is not good news for Jabe. Jabe had felt Alan might just be the anchor in life he has been searching for but the 'writing on the wall' is all too clear.

The most grounded person in Jabe's life is Laila, his friend and confidante since school. When he senses something is very wrong on Devil's Rock, it's Laila he turns to. He asks her to find out as much as she can about three suspicious deaths that occurred on the lighthouse station towards the end of the previous century. What Laila discovers makes for horrific reading.

Much of the horror genre today seems to pursue gratuitous sensationalism - shock for shock's sake rather than the sake of the story. *Satan's Lamp*, on the other hand, provides the reader with abundant 'Hammer' atmosphere, edge-of-the-seat excitement and arresting insight into the inner lives of people, past and present. The horror serves the story and not vice versa.

My own career in film, television and theatre has explored many different subjects over the years, but I find time and time again that the most popular medium is the macabre. I have been to many horror conventions and I'm always amazed at the cross section of people who frequent them. Everyone seems devoted to this dark side of entertainment and many are immensely knowledgeable about the history and development of the subculture. I'm sure that all who now turn the pages of *Satan's Lamp* - and surrender to the story - will not be disappointed.

Linda Hayden

Come away, O human child!
To the waters and the wild
With a faery, hand in hand,
For the world's more full of weeping
Than you can understand.

THE STOLEN CHILD, W B YEATS

Jabe sees the kitchen knife on the floor.
The handle feels cold, deathly.

chapter one

i

Thursday 14th October 1976

A gang of ten-year-old boys. A dilapidated alley between low-rise London flats. The boys are novice alphas - hungry for conflict - setting out to 'prove' themselves through force of numbers. Once they worked themselves up enough to knock an old woman over -

Her groceries scatter across the pavement. The boys kick the punnets of fruit and detergent boxes into the path of the oncoming traffic, and point and shout as the cars run over them.

Once they threw bricks at a window and shouted abuse - borrowed from their parents - at the Pakistani family inside. In happier circumstances, the gang's leader would

17

have been a hardworking, well-adjusted kid. But Tony was one of the Marsdens. He came from a family of bullies. He was bullied at home and so he cast around for the softest target at school - to 'get his own back'. Jabe Walker was small and so obvious prey. Tony stood a full two inches taller and right now -

He has the smaller boy pinned against the wall - Tony's grubby fingernails are digging into the soft skin under the boy's jaw. He's sneering in the boy's face. He's forcing Jabe's head backwards, twisting it sharply so he can scrape the skin of his scalp along the brickwork. Jabe's face is hot with tears.

'Poofter! Poofter! Poofter!' The chanting from the rest of the gang grows louder and louder. Tony jabs the boy in the solar plexus and there, he's doubling over. Now Jabe feels a fist slam down hard on his back between his shoulder blades and his cheek is suddenly caressing the tarmac.

'Look in his bag,' from one of the boys.

Tony's fingers close around the strap on Jabe's satchel.

'No, please!'

Tony tips up the satchel. Out fall chewed felt tips, *Five Go to Mystery Moor* and the latest issue of *Soldier*, all like so much debris at a crash site. Tony studies the front of the magazine for a moment: two Native Americans in a Red Cross helicopter. He flicks through the pages roughly then curls the magazine into a baton and beats Jabe over the head with it.

'Fairies don't like soldiers, you like dollies.'

The other boys are hollering their approval.

'It's for my dad,' Jabe replies. 'Give it back.'

Tony unfurls the magazine and begins tearing the pages up. The torn strips flutter down over Jabe like sad rain, like snow.

'There you go, nancy boy. Take it home to daddy now.'

ii

Jabe's father joined the army straight from school. He worked hard and managed to rise to the rank of lieutenant. In the end his temper wrecked his career. He was dishonourably discharged - allegations of bullying, assault and victimisation. Without the army he was rudderless. He was moody and unpredictable, venting his frustration on his wife and son. He worked at low-paid jobs: belligerent caretaker, belligerent delivery driver, belligerent car park attendant. His anger was never contained for long. He was dismissed from every job for violent arguments with co-workers, members of the public, anyone. For the past three months he had been holding down a job as a belligerent hospital porter (at least the anaesthetised - or the dead - don't argue back).

Jabe crossed the small rectangle of garden in front of the house. The garden was always neat but the door's ocean-green paint was fading and blistering now. Inside, the air was thick with the smell of roasting meat and the kitchen windows were blinded by cataracts of steam. His father was sitting at the dining table, scrutinising the gas bill flattened against the Formica. His mother stood at the stove, slicing vegetables.

'Hello almost-birthday-boy,' she said. 'Big day tomorrow. Did you have a good day at school?'

'Yeah.' He glanced quickly at her then put his satchel

on a chair and fiddled with the buttons on his coat. He didn't look at his father.

'What's up?' his mother asked.

'Nothing.'

'So, what did you do today?'

'Oh, the usual stuff,' he said.

'Anything worth mentioning?'

'Mr. Perry said me and Amanda were top of the class for reading.'

'That's wonderful, Jabe. What happened to your cheek?'

'I fell over in the playground.'

'Let me see.'

'Mum!'

Jabe pulled off his coat. He wanted to get upstairs, lock the door, hide under the bed clothes.

'Jabe, come here.' His father said slowly. 'Where's my magazine?'

Jabe held his coat in front of him like a shield. He felt a familiar urgency in his abdomen: he wanted to pee.

'Jabe, I'm asking you a question.' The boy was like a bird hypnotised by a snake. 'You did get it, didn't you?'

'Yes.'

Rufus Walker wrapped his huge paddle of a hand around his son's slim wrist.

'Then where is it?'

'Something happened, daddy.'

'Where's the magazine?'

'In my satchel.'

'Get it out, then.'

'Something happened.' Jabe's whisper was almost inaudible.

'Get it out.'

20

Jabe fumbled with the buckles and held up a handful of torn pages. His father stood up, the legs of his chair crying out against the lino. 'What the fuck have you done to my magazine?'

Jabe meant to reply but the words wouldn't come. Rufus grabbed him by the shoulders and shook him. The torn paper spilled out of his hands onto the floor still like so much rain, like snow.

'I'm asking you a question, Twiggy.' Jabe hated the nickname. 'Twiggy' meant 'too skinny for a proper boy', 'too fey', 'too weak to be my son'. Rufus Walker was shouting now. It was going to happen again. The pressure cooker was going to blow.

'It wasn't my fault. This boy… He ripped it all up.' Jabe began to cry.

'And why did he do that, Twiggy? Because you don't know how to stand up for yourself!' Rufus jabbed a finger at his son's chest. Jabe's mother, stock-still at the stove, was crushing the tea towel between her fingers.

'Please Rufus, don't,' she said gently.

'Shut up, Maggie.' Rufus Walker's face was livid and awful. He pulled his son up by the arms and drove him over the table then yanked up his shirt and pinched him repeatedly in the stomach, twisting and reddening the skin.

'You stupid…useless…little…pansy. Little bitch.'

'Leave him alone, Rufus. Please. It's not his fault.'

'I told you to shut up.'

Then Jabe wet himself.

Now it is happening again. He is grabbing his wife by the throat. She tries to cry out, but all that's heard is a

21

hollow rasping sound. He's smacking her head against the cupboard door and blood appears in a curious half moon shape over her right eye. He stabs a short sharp punch into her shoulder then returns to Jabe, pulling him up by the collar of his school shirt.

'I'll snap your bones, Twiggy. You useless little bitch.'

He strikes the boy again. Now Maggie is using her whole weight to drag her husband away from the child. He reaches back and rips out a clump of her hair. He jabs her with his elbow. He wraps his hands around her throat. She splutters and fights back. Fights less. Jabe sees her eyes rolling and closing, her face turning bloodless. Strange noises are gurgling in her throat now and saliva is dribbling from her slackened lips. But she is still alive.

Jabe sees the kitchen knife on the floor. The handle feels cold, deathly. He closes his eyes as the knife is sliding into his father. Rufus gasps and arches his back, letting go of Maggie. Blood is spreading quickly across his back and it's like a map of the world. He staggers briefly, looking as if he will fall, then he rocks on his heels towards Jabe, closing the massive palm of his hand around Jabe's nose and mouth. Now he is clamping down on the boy's jaw. Jabe hears his father's breath rattling in his throat. Blood appears between his father's lips like a second tongue then he lets out a long sigh and dies.

Impossibly, he's dead.

Jabe looked down at his father's motionless body and his own bloodstained hands. He was still holding the knife.

*Nicky's eyes shone mischievously
behind his John Lennon spectacles.*

chapter two

i

Friday 17th December 1982

'You don't belong here, Paki.' Tony Marsden shoves
Laila hard but she stands her ground. Her sloe-black hair
is cut short and emphasises a fine and resolute profile.

'Go home to Paki land,' Tony jabs his thumb towards
Jabe, 'and take your poofy friend with you.'

'It's called Pakistan,' Laila sighs. 'And I'm not from
there. I'm from India.'

'Same difference, you all stink of curry.' Tony glances
triumphantly at his sidekicks, then sticks his foot out,
slicing Laila's legs from under her. 'Everyone knows Pakis
can't fight.'

25

Jabe helped Laila up. 'I'm sorry,' he said.

'It's not your fault. Tony Marsden gets away with too much at this place.'

'That's because Callaghan just looks the other way.'

'He looks the other way when Tony bullies you too.'

The last lesson of the week was double chemistry. 'Greasy Reeder' (Arnold Reeder) was Jabe's least favourite teacher: middle-aged, spindly, elaborate comb-over - you get the picture. No one will forget the time a sticky tendril escaped as he was leaning over a bunsen burner. Greasy jerked his head up sharply just in time and the wayward strand fell neatly back into place - the stuff of legend. Laila was one of Reeder's favourite pupils because she was good at science. He made no attempt to conceal his contempt for Jabe - his little asides ('You need to hold the test tube at an angle, dear.') made it clear Greasy thought him inadequate as a scientist and a man. When the bell rang, Jabe and Laila joined the scramble to get off the school grounds. Every Friday they paused for a moment outside the gates, taking in the sounds and smells of life outside, and the fabulous promise of freedom. Two whole days of manumission. No Tony Marsden, no Greasy Reeder. They worked out how many hours stood between Friday's delirious exit and Monday's subdued return. Sixty-five hours or, as Jabe called it, 'the glorious sixty-five'.

Jabe pulled his jacket closer against the chill and realised how glad he was to know Laila. On the outside she seemed unaffected by her classmates' casual and continual racism but sometimes he felt her flinch inside a little. He liked to think he and Laila might have been brother and sister in another life, on another planet.

Laila's parents moved to Leytonstone from the Punjab in 1968. Their pebble-dashed terrace was crowded with five children - four boys and Laila, the 'baby' sister. Two of the boys were getting married soon and would be moving out. Laila was both the baby and the rebel of the family. She defied her mother and often felt the back of her father's hand.

'What's got into you?' She asked as they walked home from school together. 'You've hardly been the best company today.'

'I know,' Jabe said blankly.

'You can tell me. We're supposed to be mates.'

'My mum died three years ago today.'

'I'm a crap friend. I should've remembered.'

'You're the best friend I've got.'

'Actually, I'm the only friend you've got,' Laila said. Then after a moment: '*E.T.* is on at the Woodford ABC. Or we could try and sneak in to *Creepshow*?'

'I don't think I'd be much fun.'

'It's a cinema, Jabe. We've only got to sit there and watch.'

'Maybe we could go on Saturday? If I can scrape the money together.'

'I'll treat you,' said Laila. 'I'm Indian, we're made of money.'

The court placed Jabe at Cobden after his mother died - after pancreatic cancer finished what Jabe's father had started. It was a little further on from Laila's. The High

Street was a jumble of takeaways, discount shops, a grimy laundrette and the road was bright with rush-hour headlights picking out the first flakes of sleet. Jabe spotted another Cobden boy coming out of the off licence: 'Nicky, what did you get?'

'What d'you think?' Nicky teased open his jacket to reveal a bottle of Famous Grouse. 'I just liberated this little baby.' Nicky's eyes shone mischievously behind his John Lennon spectacles. He was slender, but not thin, and supremely sure of himself, which made him stand out from the other boys. For some reason that Jabe didn't quite understand, Nicky had chosen to take him under his wing.

'D'you want some?' Nicky produced a couple of Aeros. 'I liberated these too.'

'Your place or mine?'

'Yours.'

Being sixteen meant Jabe and Nicky had certain privileges at Cobden Road. The most important of these was a bedroom each while the rest of the boys slept on bunk beds in the dormitory. Jabe closed his bedroom door. Nicky took a drink from the bottle, wiped the top and handed it to Jabe. The whisky spilled down the back of his throat and he felt its effects spread through his chest. The spirit warmed him in spite of the chill in the little box room. The electric heater buzzed reassuringly on the wall but did little to warm up the room. Nicky looked at the Duran Duran and Bananarama posters on Jabe's walls.

'You've got crap taste in music, mate,' he said.

Jabe shivered. 'Why is this place always so cold?'

Nicky placed a milk-white hand over Jabe's. 'You're freezing.'

He drew Jabe gently to him. Nicky's grey school jumper

smelled good, something like warm, melting butter. Jabe hadn't been this close to another boy before. He was 'the psycho' or 'the poofter' or both and most boys at the home gave him a wide berth. Nicky was not a profound child but he had a strong sense of right and wrong. He was no sporting hero either so in some ways he was as much of an outsider as Jabe. And it was Nicky who had first introduced Jabe to the life-affirming qualities of alcohol.

'It's brass-monkeys out there tonight. Feeling any warmer?'

'A little,' Jabe didn't want Nicky to pull away.

'What's this?' Nicky turned Jabe's wrist over, examining the faded red mark.

'Leave it.' Jabe snatched his arm away.

'Looks like a deep cut.

'Just leave it.'

'Did you try to top yourself?'

Jabe didn't want to be reminded.

'Sorry. I didn't mean to stick my nose in.' Nicky said.

'It was a stupid thing.'

'Things must have been pretty bad.'

'I've learned to keep my head down. People don't pick on you, if you're invisible.'

'Does it work?'

'Not really.'

'Sometimes I think you just need someone to look out for you.' Nicky turned Jabe's face towards him.

Now he is pressing his lips against Jabe's. His fingers are caressing the back of Jabe's neck in firm, even strokes.

They kiss for a while.

Then Nicky is tearing at Jabe's school uniform and

taking off his own. He is pulling the covers over them and Jabe is melting into his warm buttery nakedness. Blood is pulsing, savage and deep. They taste each other hungrily until Jabe feels Nicky's passion spent in his mouth, like salt water and honey. Nicky works his lips around Jabe and now Jabe is rising towards a high plateau he has never visited before.

They lay together, the back of Jabe's head on Nicky's chest, Nicky's arm thrown lazily around him.

The world had changed forever.

He looked across the dunes to Winterton lighthouse, a stone guardian above the endless, agitated sea.

chapter three

i

Friday 26th June 1987

The second test match at Lord's was rained off for three days and the first day of Wimbledon was a soggy disappointment leaving queueing punters sodden and gloomy. 'Flaming June' was officially a washout.

The tiny flint cottage stood at the end of a row. The back gardens all faced out towards the high dunes bordering Winterton beach. The sky threatened rain as the two men unloaded their cases from the car. Jabe Walker, now twenty, was still slight for his age with a kind and boyish face. The other man was much older with the first strands of silver showing in his dark hair. Ian Brody wore a tweed jacket and corduroys. This gave him the air of a public school master, which he wasn't.

The holiday cottage was modest and functional in stark contrast to the modern flat the couple shared in east London. They settled into the little cottage quickly and methodically, under Ian's direction. They worked out the hot water system, loaded bread, milk, eggs, bacon into the fridge and hung their clothes in the wardrobe. Jabe lay out on the mattress, testing its firmness. No lumps, no springs to prod you in the back. He smiled at Ian, an invitation to lie down next to him. Ian remained standing at the foot of the bed.

'You chose well,' Jabe said, looking around at the room: pinch-pleat curtains, pine chest of draws with porcelain mallards sitting on ornately embroidered cloth. 'It's a nice place. Very countryfied. Very different from the flat.'

Ian stared out of the window. 'It's not bad. It'll be nice to have some peace and quiet for a week.'

'We might even get a swim in. If the weather improves.'

'Maybe. I've got a few things I have to do this week.' Ian moved to the door, his body a portrait of discomfort. 'I'll put the kettle on.'

Jabe didn't follow. He lay back and stared at the ceiling, thinking about the journey up to Norfolk in Ian's second-hand Saab. Heavy downpours had slowed the traffic to a crawl. They had been on edge the whole drive, Ian constantly questioning whether Jabe was reading the map correctly. Ian was a facts and figures man, an accountant, always precise and, sometimes, just a little too tightly wound. They had been dating for six months but it was obvious he was already bored with Jabe and on the lookout for the next unclaimed stray. Jabe was surprised when Ian suggested a holiday on the coast. Perhaps he was feeling guilty about something he'd done - or was about to do:

the awkward 'dear John' conversation; the 'it's me not you' speech. Jabe still wondered if he'd ever be able to trust another man. At first, Ian ticked a lot of boxes. He was older, established, experienced. Jabe thought he might help him set everything back to zero but benign father figures didn't really work out, at least not for Jabe. Heroes were a storybook fiction, a sweet little lie dreamed up to make youngsters feel safe at night.

ii

Deep below the surface of the sea, human blood changes from red to green. Go deeper still and it turns to black. On Winterton beach, the sea swells were ending their long migrations, driven by a fierce squalling wind, heaving themselves up onto the sand. The sea's song was monotonous, a dirge. The sky was puddle-grey. The only soul on the beach was Jabe. He looked across the dunes to Winterton lighthouse, a stone guardian above the endless, agitated sea. The lighthouse was a burly soldier with a stern eye on the aggressive tide of Winterton Ness, once described as the most dangerous headland between Scotland and London.

Jabe's imagination was caught by the tower's apparent strength. It stood alone against nature. The small greyish-white keepers' cottages were clustered round it for protection. He thought of his own need for sanctuary. He thought of Nicky but he was ancient history now. Jabe felt the wind biting hard. He buttoned up his jacket and walked purposefully along the beach. It was starting to drizzle as he reached the little cottage but he still paused as he slid the key in the lock.

Ian had immersed himself in work most of the week. 'I just have to get these few bits done but you don't have to wait around. Have a walk, take in the sea air. We'll go somewhere nice for dinner, I promise.' Whenever they did go out though, what little they had to say to each other was separated by agonising silences. Jabe couldn't remember how they'd got to this point.

Ian was poring over balance sheets in the sitting room. The cottage was far too small for a couple having problems.

'You're back early.' Ian didn't look up from his paperwork. The silver in his hair caught in the lamp light.

'I need to ask you something.'

Ian took off his glasses and sighed. 'I've got a lot to do.'

'This won't take long.'

Ian folded his arms.

'How do you become a lighthouse keeper?'

'I don't know, ring directory enquiries.'

Jabe moved to go.

'Where did this idea come from?' Ian asked.

'I saw the lighthouse from the beach,' Jabe replied.

iii

'You're mad. Off your bloody rocker,' Laila said between sips of coffee. 'What do you want to go and live on a bloody lighthouse for?'

'You don't live there. You do a month 'on' and a month 'off'.'

'I still think you're a bloody nutter.'

'It'll be good for me. Being away from everything.'

'You can't spend your life hiding, Jabe, whatever life's

36

thrown at you in the past. Now's the time you should be putting your life together. Maybe go to college. Have some fun. You're nice-looking. You've got a nice boyfriend.'

'Nice boyfriend and me have split.'

'I never liked him!' Laila laughed. 'And he was ancient.'

'He's thirty-five.'

'Way too old for you.'

'Turned out I was just another one of his lost causes.'

'You should have stuck with Nicky,' Laila said.

'Nicky decided he preferred girls.'

'I think I might prefer them too after the endless losers mum keeps trying to marry me off to.'

'You're way too much of a club kid to settle down.'

'Try telling my mum that. Actually, don't. All hell would break loose.'

Jabe saluted.

'So, when's the interview for the lighthouse gig?'

'Tomorrow morning.'

Laila and Jabe drank a lot of Lambrusco that night.

iv

The next morning Jabe's mouth felt like he'd been chewing on his own tee shirt. He drank tap water from a cracked tea cup he'd found under a pile of dirty plates. After uni, Laila had got a job at an ad agency, Crawfords, in Paddington ('Yes, we do make crackers...') and she had found a nice-ish flat share with Mindy, another girl from the office.

Jabe meanwhile had gone from one dead-end job to another. At times he felt blanked out from the world. Being with Ian had changed things - for a while - but

Laila was right: he needed to get his head straight, and working on a lighthouse with no distractions seemed like it might help.

The sun had painted Wanstead's streets yellow as he made his way to the station. The underground platform was packed with commuters and Jabe squeezed onto the train next to a middle-aged brickie: grubby tee, torn Levis, a copy of *The Sun* stuffed in his back pocket. He smelled of cigarettes. As the carriage rumbled into the tunnel, the lights flickered and went out. Pitch dark. Nobody reacted. Jabe changed at Mile End and took the District Line towards Tower Hill.

As he approached the pristine facade of Trinity House, butterflies danced in his belly. Trinity House was quiet as a municipal library with models of lighthouses, shipping lane maps and coastal charts. He completed a short maths and literacy test and then the interview began.

The man eyed him philosophically across an oversized desk. 'Not everyone is cut out to work on a lighthouse, and we're wending our way towards automation. But there are still some opportunities for someone young with no dependents.'

Jabe shifted in his chair. 'I really want to join. I do want to be a lighthouse keeper.'

'People often think it's exciting, pitting oneself against the elements and all that. An adventure. But it's a tough life. It's a harsh environment to work in and challenging from a social point of view: three men, cooped up together for a month - or more, if the weather closes in.'

The lighthouse, solid and dependable like a burly soldier keeping watch.

'I don't think that would be a problem for me.'

'Do you know much about the service?'

The tower's apparent strength, standing alone against nature.

'The service has a statutory duty to keep the lights showing, safeguarding shipping and seafarers.'

'Very good. I have to say, you look a little on the underweight side. Are you fit and healthy?'

'I'm not overweight but I don't think I'm underweight either.'

'Hmm. And mentally. Are you healthy in that respect?'

'I think so.'

A lie.

The interviewer gave Jabe a serious look: 'What I'm really asking you, young man, is do you have what it takes? In modern parlance: do you have the balls for the job?'

Useless little bitch.

'Yes I do!'

The man sat back. 'All right, Mr. Walker. Let's see how you get on. Welcome to the service.'

v

In less than twenty-four hours, Jabe was on his way to Harwich depot for a week's initial keeper training. He learned Morse Code, semaphore and how to operate a radio beacon. He found Morse Code laborious. Cooking was made a greater priority than he'd expected. He learned how to bake bread, an essential skill on a lighthouse, he was told. On his penultimate day, he received notice of his first posting. A month as a supernumerary keeper at St. Catherine's Lighthouse on the Isle of Wight. Jabe read up on its history: building work began on the light in 1795 but stopped soon after because the hillside was so often shrouded in mist. The eighty-nine foot tower was finally completed in 1840 by the engineers James Walker and Alfred Burgess. During a bombing raid in 1943, three lighthouse keepers took shelter in the engine house next to the tower but a direct hit killed them instantly. The main tower had a light characteristic of one white flash, repeated every five seconds. A second, smaller tower, was built in the 1930s to house the fog horn. Jabe was glad his first posting was to a mainland station. He was looking forward to long summer walks between watches.

vi

The sky was a pure sapphire blue with the day's first foamy clouds gliding in from the west. Jabe walked out past the Head Light Keeper's house: its curved front and round-headed window faced due east to the rising sun. He made his way along the sun-warmed cliffs and stretched out on the grass, watching sheep graze in the meadows beyond. His first fortnight had gone well and, if that continued, he should complete his month's probation with a good report from the Principal Keeper. The afternoon was frankly hot. A hot breeze rolled over the clifftop and rustled the dry grasses. He opened his rucksack and took out pen and paper. He had been meaning to write to Laila for ages. He started with a description of where he was, the grass swaying lazily, the warm sunshine. Then his eyes began to feel heavy, his breathing slowed.

The octagonal tower of the lighthouse station stood out white in the distance, washed whiter still by the high sun. The sky was a perfect, merciless aquamarine. Insects buzzed in the heavy air. A pause as if the world were holding its breath. Then a sudden rushing sound like the sound of dry thunder.

Now Jabe sees the source of the thunder: sheep charging blindly across a wide field. The noise is appalling. Something is lying alone in the middle of the grass. The sheep's entrails are everywhere, torn out by a wild animal, a wild dog perhaps. He walks over to the carcass. Bluebottles buzz around the opening in the animal's side, and crawl in and out of the empty eye sockets. The air is clotted with the smell of blood. Jabe turns away and sees someone standing in the corner of the field. His father.

'Little bitch. Little Twiggy. I'll snap your fucking bones.'

Jabe sat up. The sheep were grazing gently in the field. The breeze was running hot still over the cliffs.

He started back to the lighthouse, unable to shrug off the dream. Sam, the PK, was clearing away lunch. 'Your stew's in the fridge, for whenever you want it.'

'Thanks.'

'You look like you've just found something crawling in your dinner.'

'I fell asleep on the cliffs and had a strange dream,' Jabe said. 'That's all.'

'It's the tiredness - gets to us all. Maybe you should get your head down for a while now. You'll be back on at four.'

'No, I'll get some sleep later, before the watch starts.'

There are no recreational facilities on a working lighthouse. Keepers have to amuse themselves in their free time, of which there isn't much at any rate. Men keep busy according to their own tastes. Jabe went to his room and fished out his dog-eared copy of *Giovanni's Room*, a going-away present from Laila. There were few books on the lighthouse and he was already on his second reading of *Giovanni*. The sun streamed reassuringly into the keepers' cottage. Laila had been right, as always. It was time to build a life somehow. There was no need to feel afraid anymore.

For the remainder of his time at St. Catherine's, Jabe dedicated himself unstintingly to his work. The worst part was the endless cleaning schedule: mopping the tower from top to bottom as well as the keepers' accommodation. As he got used to his duties, he noticed his body toning up: his thigh and calf muscles were more solid from climbing flights and flights of stairs. His appetite doubled but he quickly burned off any excess calories. He took to jogging to keep fit and improve his stamina.

At the end of his month's probation, Trinity House arranged temporary lodgings in Cromer, Norfolk. He paid his way by doing odd jobs around the landlady's ramshackle boarding house. And he finally finished that letter to Laila. For his second posting, he was to go to Penzance. Devil's Rock, known to the locals as Satan's Lamp, was one of the most uninviting stations in the service. A hundred and forty-foot structure, fifteen miles south-west of Lizard Point, alone in the driving swells where the English Channel opened out to the Atlantic Ocean.

'Little bitch! Little Twiggy! I'll snap your bones, you worthless piece of shit.'

Jabe woke up and his breath was coming hard and quick. The room was cold and smelled of damp. Ivy Cottage Guest House wasn't the greatest accommodation in Penzance, but it was the most affordable. He swung his legs over the bed and rested his head in his hands for a moment. The alarm read 7.12am. He grabbed his towel and went down the narrow hallway to the bathroom. He turned on the shower and lukewarm water dribbled over his neck and back.

Autumn had swaggered in overnight bringing cold winds and rain. The early-morning streets were grey and wet. The taxi driver loaded Jabe's holdall into the boot of his worn-out Ford Sierra. Jabe clicked his seatbelt as the car lurched away from the kerb, U2's *The Unforgettable Fire* playing loudly on the radio.

'So, Devil's Rock?'

'Yeah.'

'First time?'

'First time on Devil's Rock.'

'Where were you stationed before?'

'St. Catherine's on the Isle of Wight.'

'Is that a rock tower?'

'Mainland.'

'Quite comfortable then? Room to stretch your legs.'

'I guess.'

'Is this your first time on a rock?'

'Yes.'

The driver gave him a peculiar smile.

'I wouldn't want your job. Not for all the tea in China.'

'It takes a certain type of person, I suppose.'

'It takes a certain type of person to set foot on Devil's Rock.' He paused for effect. 'The rock is haunted.'

Jabe laughed.

'There's something not quite right there. It's in the skin of the place. A few years back, a lad about your age died there. Jumped from the gallery just two weeks into his posting.'

Jabe saw the tower, the rocks, the wrecked body, quickly followed by an image of himself falling. Over-identification, he thought to himself, then drove the thought from his mind.

'That's awful,' he managed to say. 'Does anyone know why?'

'He said something was watching him. Like I said, the place is haunted.'

Neither of them spoke for a while. The driver realised he might have gone too far, so he said, 'There are normally two keepers to a relief. Where's the other one?'

'He's meeting me at Saint Just.'

The car rattled on between rain-sodden fields. Trees rose overhead, yellow and umber. The Sierra's wipers trapped leaves between the bonnet and the scuttle, sometimes scraping a dead leaf across the windscreen before the wind took it again.

St. Just Airport was small, used mainly for flights to the Isles of Scilly. Jabe checked his watch: fifteen minutes before the chopper was due to leave. The driver pulled up in front of the Trinity House store room where keepers collected their red plastic food boxes, loaded with provisions for the month ahead. As Jabe got out of the car, a man came hurrying towards him. He was tall, probably late thirties, sandy haired with improbably blue eyes.

'Jabe Walker?'

'That's me.'

'Alan Blake. I'm the other keeper. We need to go right now. Something's happened on Devil's Rock.'

*A thick bank of cloud bubbled up off
the shoreline, dark as whale skin.*

chapter four

i

The cabin rocked from side to side as the Bell 222 climbed into the rain-heavy sky. It flew low, skirting the edge of the town, then turned sharply past rows of thin terraced cottages, out over waterlogged grasslands to the open sea. A thick bank of cloud bubbled up off the shoreline, dark as whale skin.

'What's happened?' Jabe said.

'One of the keepers has gone missing,' Alan replied. 'We'll know more when we get there.'

The whitewashed buildings of Sennen Cove passed underneath them. The water in the bay was rough, the wind riding hard against the tide.

'You're very young,' Alan said. 'How long have you been in the service?'

'A couple of months.'

Alan looked away as the helicopter banked to the right then pushed onwards, encircled by degrees by the vast grey field of the Atlantic. A life raft took up the seat next to the pilot. In the back, Alan's tall frame and long legs left little space for Jabe. The nose of the helicopter pointed determinedly towards the mass of water ahead. Jabe felt the tiny aircraft was really no match for the sea. Survival training seemed like meagre preparation for the real thing: upside down in a freezing swimming pool, grappling to release his safety belt in 'the dunker', a cage contraption meant to simulate a chopper ditched at sea.

Devil's Rock is the most remote station in the service. In heavy storms, waves easily top the tower, smashing first into its granite flank then climbing its full length in seconds. The tower rocks slightly, making a sound like crunching gravel. As the wave hits, the air pressure spikes, making your ears pop and letting you know that just beyond the storm shutters is a colossal volume of water. Jabe closed his eyes and gripped his seat as the helicopter battled against the gathering wind. The leather was cold against his skin. Alan tapped him on the shoulder. They must have been in the air about thirty minutes.

'There she is,' he said.

Ahead was the tapering tower perched on one corner of a spiky outcrop of lava rock. The entire rock was only about eighteen hundred feet across, but looked redoubtable amidst the relentless onrush of the sea. The helipad jutted out over the lantern, giving the whole structure the look of a thin grey mushroom with the cap sliced off.

'We'll need to make this quick,' the pilot said. 'Search

48

and Rescue are right behind us.'

Alan gave the thumbs up to the pilot and winked at Jabe. 'Interesting first day.'

Jabe smiled weakly.

The helicopter banked left and spiralled rapidly down to the helideck. As Alan and Jabe unloaded their bags and red food boxes, the wind ricocheted across the platform. They passed their gear through the hatch into the lantern gallery where it was stacked by the departing keeper. After exchanging quick greetings with the new arrivals, he hurried up the ladder to the waiting chopper. It rose away from the platform as if picked up by the wind before turning sharply and striking out again across the open sea. Jabe watched it wavering in the air, toyed with by the wind. He was glad it was a whole month before he had to make the trip again.

ii

Cyrus Jones shook hands with the new arrivals. Jabe guessed the keeper was about ten years older than Alan. He wore a goatee moustache that grizzled the sides of his chin and his long straggly hair was pulled back in a ponytail. He was gaunt and pale, and the telltale lines of a smoker were starting to form around his lips. It was cold in the tower and the cold felt worse because of the damp. Cyrus left them to unpack their things in the sleeping quarters. The room was cramped - no more than twelve feet in diameter - with 'banana bunks', curved beds lining the semi-circular walls. Jabe and Alan had to manoeuvre carefully around one another on the small circle of floor. The confined space made Jabe aware of Alan: he noticed pale blond brows above bright blue eyes, a handsomely assertive face and, as he brushed past him, skin with a scent like jasmine or sweet apples. They folded knitted jumpers, tee shirts, socks and underpants into drawers. Jabe glanced furtively at Alan's underclothes. Then they chose bunks. Jabe took the top one, directly above Alan. He felt like he was ten years old again on holiday with his parents in Cornwall. They had taken him to stay at a guesthouse just outside Truro. He could still remember the smell of moth balls in the wardrobes and Peggy, the landlady with daffodils on her apron, frying bacon and eggs in the morning. He loved having the large, whitewashed room, with its Great Western Railway posters, all to himself. And he always hurried to the top bunk, pulling the curtain across behind him. Pretending he was on a spaceship in suspended animation, like an astronaut in *Planet of the Apes*, far out in the galaxy; somewhere nothing in the world, not even his father, could touch him.

The Sikorsky labouring in the wind announced the arrival of the Coast Guard. The helicopter circled the tower several times before expanding its search further out over the water. Alan zipped up his empty holdall and stored it overhead. 'I'll see you downstairs,' he said. As soon as he heard Alan's footsteps receding, Jabe took two bottles of Famous Grouse out of his bag - in case of emergencies - and hid them in the drawer under his tee shirts and jumpers.

'What happened to the missing keeper?' Alan was asking Cyrus as Jabe came into the living quarters.

'We were cleaning seaweed off the landing stage. Bill Norton, our Principal Keeper, was out there with the chloride of lime. It was most likely the last time we could clear it before winter and he was keen to get started. Paddy - that's the keeper you've just relieved - was getting his protective gear on. I was lookout.'

Jabe's training had been full of warnings about chloride of lime - *a highly toxic substance that will burn unprotected skin* - and the need for a lookout at all times. The lookout kept watch for any unexpected wave large enough to sweep a man off the landing stage. If the lookout saw anything untoward, he signalled the other men and they made for the designated safe spot.

'Paddy called to me from inside.' Cyrus continued. 'I took my eyes off Bill for a split second. I don't know where the wave came from. Knocked Bill off his feet and he was gone.'

'Was he wearing his life jacket?' Alan asked.

'We followed procedure,' Cyrus shot back, taking Alan's question as criticism. 'But when we went out to look for him, there was no sign. Nothing.'

'But the jacket would have kept him afloat.'

'Well it didn't. It was like the sea had been waiting to claim him.'

'Or, more likely, a freak wave,' Alan said. 'Or the wash from a container ship miles out. It happens.'

'This wasn't like that. Wasn't like anything I've ever seen before,' Cyrus said. 'I was supposed to be going home today on that chopper with Paddy. With Bill gone I've got to stay behind.' He seemed more concerned about losing shore leave than losing a colleague. Jabe decided he didn't like Cyrus. Even if Cyrus and Bill Norton didn't get along, the man was still missing, probably dead, and he would have family and friends back on the mainland.

51

Jabe looked out of the small rusty window. The Sikorsky was still droning in the distance, widening its search for Norton further and further. Cyrus handed out cups of tar-coloured tea. He packed tobacco into a Rizla paper and then went over the roster: Alan would take the afternoon watch from noon to 8pm. Cyrus would split the middle watch with him from 8pm to 4am. Jabe would take morning watch next day from 4am to noon.

'Lunch is at half past twelve every day,' Cyrus said, fishing three crabs out of the fridge. 'We caught these beauties yesterday.' The crab shells made a queasy cracking sound as he twisted the claws and legs free of the body. Then he pushed out the whole body section with his thumbs. To Jabe it sounded like someone's neck snapping.

Alan and Jabe unpacked their food boxes into the lockers: tins of peas, sweetcorn, baked beans and packets of spaghetti. Into the freezer: fresh lamb, beef and chicken. A constant whispering sounded between the stairwells and the windows thrown open against the relentless condensation.

'What do you think of our comrade?' Alan asked.

'Not the nicest guy.'

'Callous bastard if you ask me,' Alan spoke quietly. 'He's well-known throughout the service: Spooky Jones they call him. He's supposed to be into some wacko stuff.'

'Like?'

'UFOs, conspiracy theories, the occult and all that jazz. The more wacko, the better, they say.'

Jabe laughed. 'You're not a believer?'

'Not me, mate. But old Spooky reckons its all for real. I think he's full of crap. He's spooked some of the younger guys. Hence the name. Just be careful around him. Don't let him get inside your head.'

'How long have you worked in the service?' Jabe asked.

'Fifteen years next month. I joined when I was just a kid. Now we're a dying breed. In about ten years' time there won't be any keepers. Computers will be running everything. It'll be like *A for Andromeda*.'

'What?'

'An old TV show. They built a great big computer and it tried to take over the world. It could take over your mind, control your body. It was a great show. Before your time - 1960s.'

'Are you married, Alan?'

'I got hitched when I was sixteen - two kids by the time I was your age. Now they're grunting teenagers and I'm glad to get away from them for a month at a time.'

They heard the Sikorsky roar past the open window. Jabe looked out to see it powering back towards the mainland.

The search for Bill Norton was over.

The stairwell was brutally cold. The beating of the generator competed with the sound of the sea outside.

chapter five

i

Jabe ran into the kitchen holding a brown paper bag. He took out three little cupcakes; one for him, one for mum and one for dad. His father was alone at the table. 'Look daddy. Look what I made at Laila's.' His father took all three cakes in his hand and slowly crushed them, the crumbs dropping over the table and onto the floor.

'Boys don't make cakes, Jabe.' Rufus grabbed his son by the collar. 'Boys don't make fucking cakes.'

'Yes, daddy.'

'You should be playing with the other boys - not playing housewives with that Paki girl.' He shook his son hard - shaking some sense into him - hard and harder still.

Jabe was only seven years old.

55

Alan shaking Jabe gently. 'Time to get up,' he said. 'It's nearly 4am. Your watch, son. That must have been some dream. You were thrashing about like a madman.'

Jabe wiped sleep from his eyes. 'Just a stupid nightmare.' He got dressed and joined Alan in the living quarters. A pot of tea, steam rising from the spout, stood next to a plate of digestive biscuits. Alan filled two mugs. Tufts of dirty-blond hair fanned out from under his fisherman's cap and his jeans were frayed over one knee, revealing pale hairs, almost white. He blinked repeatedly because he was fighting to stay awake: he'd been up for almost twenty-four hours. His voice was gritty with tiredness when he spoke.

'You look pretty wiped out.' Jabe said.

'I didn't sleep so well the night before coming out here. Going straight into one-and-a-half watches is a killer. I'll be glad to get my head down.'

'Go now, I'll be okay.'

'No, I'll stay until you're bright-eyed and bushy tailed.' It was usual for the keeper coming off duty to stay with the relieving keeper for a while - to ensure he was awake and completely alert. The room was chilly and Jabe suppressed a shudder. 'Can I ask you a question, Alan?' he said. 'What do you know about the kid who killed himself here?'

'He was a greenhorn like you,' Alan said sleepily. 'Turned out he couldn't cope with being cooped up on a lighthouse. His name was Vinnie. That was it, Vinnie...'

'On the way to the airport, the taxi driver said something about Devil's Rock spooked him. He said Devil's Rock is haunted.'

'There are strange stories about almost every lighthouse

56

on the English coast,' Alan said. 'I put it all down to tiredness - that muzzy-headed feeling that comes at the end of a long watch. The mind plays tricks when these old towers start creaking and groaning in the middle of the night.' He looked at Jabe thoughtfully. 'Do you believe in ghosts?'

'I don't know. I haven't met any yet.'

Jabe began his shift, checking that the lighthouse beam was rotating correctly: the light swept blithely over the agitated sea. Next he cleared the crockery away, wiped down the kitchen surfaces and swept and washed the floor. He left the floor to dry and went to check the engine room. The stairwell was brutally cold. The beating of the generator competed with the sound of the sea outside. He checked the speed of the light on the optic speed monitor, then climbed up into the lantern itself. Like a giant crystal, the huge lamp occupied almost the entire space. Its lenses threw stray fractals of light onto the metal lattices of the astragals. The mechanism rattled irritably as it rotated.

He opened the bulkhead door to the gallery. The wind danced around him. He climbed up onto the top of the guard rail, holding on with both hands. The wind was fiercer now. He caught his breath as he looked down. A long way down, the waves crashed into the base of Devil's Rock. Vinnie must have climbed up here, Jabe thought. Vinnie must have looked down just as Jabe was looking down now. Jabe imagined Vinnie must have jumped in the early hours: in the dream time before the sun burns away the night terrors. Jabe listened to the wind singing in his ears. He felt he was nothing, less than a speck of nothing. Only his grip on the metal rail kept him from falling. He imagined the fall onto the rocks below. Blood and shattered bones swept away by the sea forever. Gone. Then he heard his name called softly. There it was again, riding on the wind, barely audible. He stepped clumsily back down onto the walkway. It must have been the wind, he thought. The wind and his imagination. But the tower was heavy now - with many unnameable things.

ii

The wind died in the night. Now sunlight reflected coolly off calm, bright water. Jabe called in the weather report to the coastguard: 'Wind west-south-west, 5-6, heavy south-westerly swell.' He filled in the log, turned off the optic and put up the blackout blinds in the lantern. Training stressed the importance of the blinds again and again: left uncovered, the optic would focus the sun's rays, damaging the internal electrics or even starting a fire.

Jabe took a break from cleaning the engine room and he found Spooky in the living quarters, smoking and drinking coffee.

'I'm going fishing on the far side of the rock,' Spooky said.

'Making the most of your day off?'

'You don't need me for anything. Might as well get out while the weather's fine.'

Jabe sat down opposite him.

'I can't believe Bill Norton drowned yesterday,' he said. 'Is it the first time someone's died on your watch?'

'Yeah.'

'You weren't here when the keeper Vinnie killed himself?'

'Yeah, I was here then.'

Jabe was unnerved by Spooky's indifference. 'What happened?' he pressed.

'Not much to tell.' Spooky took a long drag on his cigarette and regarded him with narrow, saurian eyes. 'Scrawny kid, nervous. He wasn't suited at all to being a keeper.' Spooky drew his lips back in a crooked smile. 'But I'll tell you one thing: he had the gift. He just didn't know how to use it. He knew there was something other on Devil's Rock.'

'What does that mean?'

'Something all around this place and in the waters off the rock. Something waiting, watching. You can feel it too.' Spooky talked very quietly, as if acknowledging this was a secret only the two of them shared. Jabe kept his expression blank. 'Listen, kid. If you see anything strange, it's just the tower keeping its watch.' Spooky stood up and moved to the door. 'I'll leave you to it. I won't be back till this afternoon, so stick my lunch in the fridge. I reckon you've still got plenty to do.'

iii

Alan took the mug Jabe offered him. Blondish stubble covered his neck and jaw. His chest was firm and covered with hair that continued down his stomach to his navel and the waistband of his black briefs. His nipples were pale amethyst. Jabe's senses were very keen and the feeling of closeness warmed him.

'Thanks for waking me up, mate,' Alan said. 'What's for lunch?'

'Beef stew.'

Alan seemed pleased that Spooky wasn't joining them.

The sun was higher in the sky, giving the illusion that the sea was milky white. There was no horizon. Jabe ladled the hot stew onto two plates and tore off a hunk of bread. He liked being around Alan.

'This is better than what I get at home,' Alan laughed, heaping meat and mash onto his fork.

'Your wife's not a good cook?'

Alan shook his head. 'Everything's out of a packet.'

'What about your kids? Are they still at school?'

'Andy left last year. Joined the merchant navy. John's got a year to go. Wants to leave before his A-levels.'

'Any idea what he wants to do?'

'No. He just doesn't want to be at school!' There was a resigned note in Alan's voice. After almost two decades, his marriage had become mechanical. His family life was a series of repetitive actions and predictable reactions. He was a man going through the motions in a dead-end job.

'School wasn't great for me,' Jabe said. 'I got bullied a lot.'

'Any reason in particular?' Alan's tone grew warmer.

'Any reason they could find.' Jabe said. 'I was too uncool. I was too weedy. Too gay.' His heart beat a little faster at this half-confession.

Alan laughed. 'Kids think everyone's gay.'

'Yeah, they do, don't they?'

iv

Jabe lay down on his bunk. A silverfish glided across the window sill and he squashed it without thinking.

He pulled out one of the bottles of Famous Grouse and took a couple of swigs. He lay awkwardly on the banana

60

bunk picking at the eczema on his upper arm. A little blood pooled slowly around the reddened marks. He dabbed at the wounds with a tissue until it was dotted with red. He started to think about Alan, then stopped himself. He had to get some sleep.

The final entry in the lighthouse log read: monster storm approaching, the like of which we've never seen.

chapter six

i

'It's your watch, newbie.' Jabe was still struggling to wake up as Spooky slouched out of the sleeping quarters. He stared at a point on the floor and breathed in deeply. The freezing air caught at the back of his throat. He brought his feet gingerly down onto the cold stone floor and dressed quickly and silently so as not to wake Alan. Alan was curled in the foetal position: he was several inches too tall for the curved bunk. A few inches from his feet, on a narrow shelf, lay his Seiko sports watch, a faded black leather wallet, a Silco travel alarm clock and a photograph in a silver frame smudged with finger marks. The picture showed a younger Alan on a beach somewhere. Jabe guessed the Mediterranean. Alan was very handsome. His hair was longer and bleached by the

63

sun. He was crouching on the sand with the sparkling sea stretching away endlessly behind him. A boy, about six years old, was resting on his knee and he had his arm around the waist of another boy of seven or eight. The older boy wore a Spurs football shirt and had a distant look about him, the same look as his father. There was nothing on the shelf to indicate Alan had a wife.

'It's the Devil's hour,' chuckled Spooky as he filled Jabe's mug with hot, sweet tea.

'What?' Jabe's head still swimming a little with tiredness.

'Midnight.' Spooky paused for effect. 'The witching hour. When the supernatural is at its most powerful. Ghosts appear and strange things happen. The paranormal, the unexplained. I've been interested in Devil's Rock ever since I joined the service.' Spooky added darkly. 'Always wanted to be posted here, unlike most keepers.'

'Why don't people want to come here? Because of the name?'

'Because of the Slaying. It's not something they talk about at Trinity House, specially when someone's looking for a job.'

'What's the Slaying?'

Spooky hunched forward, eager to tell a grisly tale. 'Almost a hundred and twenty-five years ago to the day, three keepers were murdered on Devil's Rock. It was the SS Adolphine, a German passenger ship, that first noticed something was wrong. On the way back from America, they passed the rock and they saw the light was out. They reported it to the German authorities and they alerted Trinity House. When a reconnaissance vessel was sent to the rock, they found the bodies of the three keepers. Each man's eyes had been pulled from their sockets. It was as if whatever killed them couldn't bear to look at its own reflection.'

'Don't you mean whoever killed them?'

'Or maybe it took their eyes for some other reason.'

The lamp over the table rocked gently in the draught, swinging discs of shadow in and out of Spooky's eye sockets so that he looked like a prop on a ghost train. Jabe got up. He'd had enough of Spooky for one night.

'I think I've woken up now. You can get to bed.'

Spooky stretched and yawned. 'I'll see you in the morning, newbie. Sure you'll be okay?' Spooky's tone was sarcastic. Jabe met his stare. And held it.

'I'll be fine, thanks.' He finished his drink then began mopping out the living quarters. He filled a bucket with warm soapy water and worked the mop but his mind kept returning to Spooky's story. Three dead men in this tower, maybe even murdered in this room.

I'll snap your bones. Little Twiggy, little bitch.

The lights in the room went out. A moment later, they came back on. Jabe left the bucket in the middle of the room and went out to the stairwell. He could hear the heavy rumbling of the generator. It was a familiar sound and it should have been comforting, but it wasn't.

He checked the console readings in the service room and hurried up to the top engine room to check on C engine. Everything seemed to be working properly, except his shadow.

Here, his shadow is standing square to him, facing him head on. Everything is wrong. Light is bending round corners. The laws of physics are suspended. Then he realises the shadow isn't his. He looks for Spooky or Alan but he's alone and now the shadow is moving in a way no shadow moves, rising, thinning into the shadow of the fog signal compressors and the engine housing.

Jabe blinked. A breeze licked the back of his neck but the windows up here were all closed. He felt as if something was crawling in the small of his back and then he felt immense fear. He returned quickly to the living quarters. He ate his meals here every day. He watched TV here with the other keepers. It should have made him feel better but it didn't. He tried to convince himself that what he'd just seen was an illusion conjured by tiredness and the poor light. But he knew it wasn't. He made himself busy, preparing the weather report: wind east-north-east, 5-6, heavy northeasterly swell. The room seemed colder, smaller. The air tasted of damp. He knew something was watching him.

ii

'Trinity House?'

'Yes, miss. I've got a message for you from Jabe Walker on Devil's Rock.' The man's voice on the end of the line was tinny and far away.

'Is everything okay?' Laila asked.

'As far as I know, miss.' The voice began reading in a disinterested monotone.

This might seem a strange thing to ask – there was a disaster on Devil's Rock – it happened in the last century – some keepers were found dead in the tower – they call it the Slaying – I want

66

to find out what really happened– specially as I'm here and this tower is a strange place – thanks for doing this – Jabe.

Laila put the receiver back in its cradle. The sun had slipped below the rooftops like an animal hiding from the hunt. From the kitchen window she saw twilight's long shadows painting shapes on the lawns around the block. Street lamps gradually flickered into life along the narrow road dotted with spreading sycamores and dark London planes. She shivered. Then she heard the front door open and her flatmate Mindy appeared. 'You look pensive. What's up?'

'Jabe wants me to find out about murders! From the nineteenth century.'

'Gruesome! Where do you start with something like that?'

'I thought the library. Can I borrow your card?'

'You really should get one of your own.'

'I always end up with a fine. And I buy enough books to keep Virago going single-handed.'

Mindy dug out the card from her coat pocket and waved it admonishingly. 'If you get any books out, make sure you take them back on time.'

'Don't worry. I won't damage your reputation.'

iii

Saturday. Rain. Laila had to collect the dry cleaning and it was her turn to do the weekly shop but here she was headed to Wanstead library: wildly austere nineteen-sixties oblong; brown brick. The librarian (brown hair, short at the ears; white safari suit) studied Laila over the top of her glasses.

67

'I'm looking for some information about lighthouses.' Laila said.

'That'll be in the reference section under 'Transportation'.'

All Laila could find were books on the history and construction of lighthouses. She thought about the name, Devil's Rock and tried 'Folklore' on a hunch. Vincent Gaddis's *Invisible Horizons* offered up plenty of stories of ghost ships and sea monsters but nothing about Devil's Rock. Similarly Charles Fort and Charles Wyllys Elliott gave detailed accounts of fish falling from the sky and the Rochester Rappings but, again, no reference to Devil's Rock. Then it caught her eye: *Strange Sea Mysteries* in gold lettering on a blood-red spine. *Strange Sea Mysteries* was full of disappearances - the American schooner, The Patriot, in 1812 and the USS Cyclops, lost in the Bermuda Triangle in 1918. And here was what she was looking for: a single page on the mysterious killing of three lighthouse keepers on Devil's Rock on the night of the 15th of October 1862.

On its voyage from New York City to Bremen, the commercial passenger liner SS Adolphine passed Devil's Rock. The crew of the Adolphine saw the tower's single multi-wick oil lamp was not lit. When the Adolphine docked several days later, this information was passed on to Trinity House.

A relief tender was sent to investigate and arrived on 24th October. The captain, Tom Wilkins, fired a flare and sounded the ship's horn. There was no response from the three keepers. The relief keeper, Charles Brentford, disembarked and entered the lighthouse. Everything was silent as he made his way upstairs by torchlight. When he reached the living quarters, he found the bodies of two of the keepers: principal keeper,

Nathaniel Smithee, and apprentice keeper, Paul Roddick. Their eyes were gone and each man's neck was broken.

Arming himself with a meat cleaver, Brentford continued his climb. At the top of the tower, something leapt out at him. He swung wildly, almost falling but it was only Mullins, the lighthouse cat. He found the third keeper, James Church, hanging from the lantern gallery. His neck was broken and his eyes, too, were missing. Brentford returned to the landing and reported what he had seen to the captain. Four sailors joined Brentford in a thorough search of the island but they could find no sign of the three men's killer. The final entry in the lighthouse log was dated 15th October. It read: 'A monster storm approaching, the like of which we've never seen.'

The London Times *speculated that the murders were committed by a lunatic, shipwrecked on the rock, and taken in by the keepers. More outlandish stories followed.* The Penny Illustrated Paper *suggested that a sea monster had attacked the men.* The Morning Post *said the Devil himself had paid a visit to the tower that night.* Witches and Demons, *Eliphas Beaufort's 1875 best-seller, placed a gateway to hell in the waters off Devil's Rock. This, Beaufort said, accounted for the mysterious disappearances of the SS Bernadette in 1865 and the SS Delphine in 1872.*

Laila closed the book and looked at the cover: an enigmatic illustration of a sea monster rising out of the ocean. The creature was allegedly seen by passengers on the SS Hydaspes sailing out of Bombay in March 1876. The author's name was Ruth Christie and the publisher, Wolfbane books, of 63 Store Street, Bloomsbury. Laila dumped her shopping in the kitchen, hung her wet raincoat in the shower to dry then looked up Wolfbane books in the telephone directory.

Friday 9th October 1987

Jabe stopped spreading raspberry jam on his toast for a moment as somebody trudged past the living quarters. He guessed it was Spooky on his way to the shower. The tiny cubicle was just off the stairwell. Spooky wasn't on duty that day but the THV Mermaid was due with fresh water and oil for the generators. All three keepers would be needed to unload the supplies. Jabe bit into his toast, licking melted butter from his fingers. His thoughts were full of missing Principal Keeper, Bill Norton. Who was mourning for him back on the mainland? He tried to put himself in Norton's shoes in the last few moments before he was swept away by the sea. Had he known he was going to die? Jabe had read about near death experiences: the woman who survived a car crash - barely - and described being outside her own body, above the wreckage, knowing her children were trapped inside but feeling no sense of panic. She reported feeling still and calm, no longer part of the living world. Had Norton felt a similar peace as the sea took hold of him? Had it felt like an inevitability, like something to be embraced, surrendered to? Jabe decided to go down to the landing platform.

He struck the undersides of the bracing bars with his hammer and heaved open the bulkhead doors. He climbed down the dog steps onto the granite landing stage where the sea chuckled against the rocks. It was hard to imagine a man being swept to his death here. The tower would have been the last thing Norton saw, disappearing below the horizon, as the current drew him swiftly out to sea. Jabe glanced up at the lantern. It took a moment, a beat, for the full horror to sink in. Then he called out, 'Oh dear God! Oh God, Oh No!' and bolted back the way he'd come.

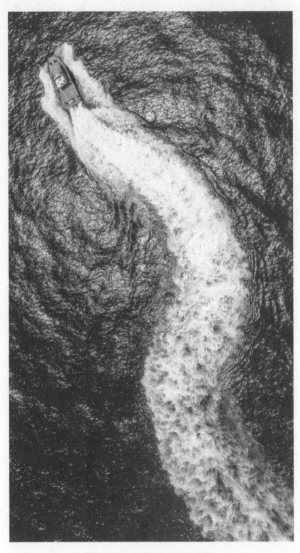

*The launch skimmed swiftly
over the water towards the landing stage.*

chapter seven

i

Jabe rushed up into the lantern, stumbling on the stairs in his panic. Alan was already there, hanging the second of the lantern's six protective blackout blinds.

'Oh Jesus,' Jabe said. 'Thanks.'

'No problem,' Alan smiled. 'Wouldn't want our old friend Spooky finding out.'

Putting up the blinds didn't take long, but it was essential. And it was always the responsibility of the keeper on morning watch.

'Thanks, Alan. I really appreciate it.'

Alan squeezed Jabe's shoulder with a firm hand. 'I figure it's my job to take care of the new boy. But don't forget again!'

His eyes were a striking blue in the morning brightness.

He held Jabe's gaze for a moment then looked away. In Alan's company, Jabe felt as if a door might be opening into some strange and lovely and unexplored territory. He let the feeling warm him, enjoying the moment for as long as it might last but he was careful to give nothing away.

'We'd better go down,' Alan said. 'The Mermaid arrives at half past twelve.'

The THV Mermaid, based at East Cowes on the Isle of Wight, was one of a small number of Trinity House supply ships. The current model, constructed by Hyundai Heavy Industries, was her fourth incarnation. Alan and Jabe found Spooky in the living quarters. Cheese on toast was bubbling under the grill. Spooky looked questioningly at Jabe. 'You went racing up the tower like a rat up a drainpipe. What was that all about?'

'Nothing.' Alan answered for Jabe.

'Didn't look like nothing.'

'Let's just drop it.'

The tension in the little kitchen spread like ink in water. Spooky stared at Alan for a few seconds then snatched the toast from under the grill and cursed because he burnt his fingers. 'Tender'll be here in thirty minutes,' he said sharply.

For a while no one spoke, which was no bad thing. Too often, the talk turned to Spooky's favourite things: unsolved murders, disappearances and hauntings. Alan had no time for what he called Spooky's 'weird shit'. Jabe found Spooky depressing, he was also curious. And, though he didn't like to admit it, a little afraid. He'd asked Laila to find out about the Slaying but he didn't want Spooky to know he took any of it seriously and he certainly didn't want Alan finding out; rational, practical

Alan. Jabe looked out of the window. Autumn sunshine lit the water. Pencil-thin clouds scribbled over the sky. The conditions were ideal for the Mermaid to land her supplies of water and fuel.

The Mermaid anchored a safe distance from the tower and the launch skimmed swiftly over the water towards the landing stage. Alan cast a heaving line to the boat. All three keepers dragged the mooring ropes from the launch and tied them to the iron rings in the landing. The launch carried oil and water, and a pumping engine. The keepers had rigged the crane ready to hoist the coil of pipe onto the landing. The tower's winch hauled the pipe the rest of the way up to the winch room and the pump started refilling the oil tanks. Next the keepers turned their attention to the water tanks at the base of the tower, re-supplying them with drinking water.

The launch was ready to return to the Mermaid. Alan knelt to untie the mooring ropes. A wave nosed the tender, causing it to roll and the mooring rope tightened unexpectedly.

Suddenly, it takes Alan's feet from under him. He smacks his head against the granite landing. His body is limp now and the tangled rope is dancing up and down and dragging him to the water's edge. Jabe leaps to grab hold of him. He holds on, but Alan's body weight is pulling the unconscious man over the side. Jabe's arm feels like it's being drawn slowly from its socket and the sea is chuckling and nodding and bobbing and licking its lips. The launch's crew realise just in time what is happening. The little boat's engines roar up and power it back towards the tower and the mooring line slackens. Jabe's strength is failing him and Alan is sliding slowly out of his arms. Then Spooky is at his side and grabs Alan and hauls him back safely onto the landing.

Jabe puts his ear close to Alan's mouth and nose. He hears a shallow breath. Another. Now another. He makes sure Alan's tongue is clear of his airway. Now he is taking Alan's head in his hands, cradling his neck, and Spooky is rotating Alan's body into the recovery position, and it is Michelangelo's Pieta with Jabe as the Virgin Mary and Alan as the fallen Christ. Jabe shouts at Spooky, 'What took you so long? You were standing right next to me when he went down.'

'I lost my footing on some weed. Took a tumble myself.'

Alan/Christ's eyes blink open. His hand moves instinctively to the back of his head. There is a little blood. Today's stigmata. The launch is just feet away from the landing, engine stuttering and one of the crew is calling across and Alan quickly waves away the offer of help. He looks up at Jabe. 'Just get me inside,' he says.

Jabe helped Alan to the living quarters while Spooky finished up on the landing. Jabe cleaned and dressed the cut and bandaged Alan's head to hold the dressing in place.

'How do you really feel?' he looked squarely at Alan. 'No macho stuff.'

Alan smiled drily. 'Like shit.'

Jabe helped Alan onto the banana bunk. He pulled the covers over his shoulders and went downstairs to get a hot water bottle. He found Spooky rolling a cigarette.

'Is he okay?' Spooky said.

'He should be all right. No thanks to you.'

'What's that supposed to mean?' Spooky was defiant.

'There wasn't any weed out there. You were cleaning the landing when Bill Norton died.' Spooky was eyeball to eyeball with Jabe. He was leaning hard into him, backing him towards the wall. He stank of tobacco.

'Don't fuck with me, newbie. I slipped over out there. Don't try and pin it on me, just because your buddy was careless. I'm acting PK on this station.' He turned towards the door. 'I'm going to check the batteries.'

Inevitably, Spooky reminded Jabe of his father. He felt the familiar urgency in his stomach. *Little Twiggy! I'll snap your fucking bones you little bitch.*

The kettle whistled brightly. Jabe filled the water bottle and took it up to Alan. Alan was sitting up in bed, propped awkwardly against the curved wall.

'You're supposed to be resting.'

'I'll be all right in a minute.'

Jabe tucked the hot water bottle under the blanket at Alan's feet.

'Thanks.' Alan said. 'Thanks for helping me out on the landing.'

'For a minute, I thought we were going to lose you.' He realised Alan was holding his arm. Neither of them dared look at the other. Then, very quietly, Alan told him to close the door.

ii

Jabe is lightheaded as Alan guides his hand towards his zipper. Jabe reaches inside, finding the waistband of Alan's briefs. He closes his fingers around Alan's hardness and draws it carefully through the opening of his jeans. Alan yields almost instantly, unable to contain his long-suppressed frustration. He pulls Jabe close and, for a split second, Jabe imagines they might kiss. Alan pushes Jabe's head down onto his chest and wraps a strong arm around him. Jabe keeps still as stone. He doesn't want to break the spell. Alan's breathing becomes slow and heavy. Then Jabe hears Spooky coming down the stairs so pulls the sheets gently over Alan, and leaves.

He dropped the bream onto the cutting board,
slicing easily into the soft, white flesh.

chapter eight

i

Out in the distance, a trawler, small as a grain of barley, rode the sea's rippling satin. Alan connected the red kite to a line and let it ride out to a distance of around seventy-five feet. The kite leapt in the air above the waves, perfect for fishing. He locked the rod, fixed a clip to the kite line's base and attached a rubber worm to the bait line. As soon as the bait was in the water, he settled his gaze on the orange cork, bobbing just above the surface, and sat back in a folding chair propped against one of the lantern's storm panes.

This was where he was meant to be. This rock in this sea. He didn't want to think about the future, about automation. And he didn't want to think about what had happened between him and the kid. He didn't want to think about AIDS - 'the gay plague' the tabloids called it. He had meant to be nice to the kid. Now he was afraid he'd started something he wouldn't be able to stop. He'd have to speak to Jabe but he could figure it out later. Now all he wanted was the lulling rumble of the waves, the smell of salt in the air, the choking calls of the seagulls nestled on the low-lying outcrops of Devil's Rock.

Alan woke up with a start, shaking his head quickly from side to side and rubbing his eyes. The wind eddied gently around the lantern but the sun's warmth still dominated. He pulled down the collar of his fisherman's coat, feeling the air cool against his neck. The orange cork dropped suddenly. He let the bait line go out then started to reel it in. A large mackerel glinted on the end of the line. It rose quickly to the top of the tower like a magical flying fish, twisting and thrashing in the clean air. He unhooked the suffocating fish and tossed it into the red food box at his feet. The excitement of the catch had woken him up properly. He had a cup winner's feeling. He caught four more fish: three bream, another mackerel. Then he stowed the line and lure, and made his way down towards the living quarters to clean and fillet the fish and bag them up for the freezer.

ii

'We should talk about what happened between us.' Jabe is standing behind Alan in the living quarters. Alan is drying the dishes and they are alone. Alan puts the tea towel down and turns around and Jabe continues: 'Are we okay? We haven't really spoken since the accident.'

'We do need to talk about it.' Alan says.

'So talk.'

There is a long silence before Alan speaks again.

'It's very difficult. We can't let anybody find out what happened.'

'I understand that but I need to know how you feel.'

Jabe had run this conversation over and over again these past few days but this was as far as he ever got. He hadn't the slightest idea how Alan really felt. The man was so held back. Their relationship was stilted now. The hope of anything more between them may have stalled but Jabe still felt longing for Alan. Loving Alan might help him overcome his fear of other people. Loving Alan might help diminish his suspicion of men and men's violence.

He finished browning minced lamb on the Belling, stirred in grated onion, carrot and garlic. He added Worcester sauce, tomato puree and a splash of red wine then spooned the mince mixture into a dish, topped it with mashed potato, and put it in the oven. He scrubbed and dried the pans. The draining board was stained and grubby; Spooky hadn't bothered to clean it on his watch. Jabe wiped it clean as new with hot, soapy water.

He mumbled an awkward greeting as he passed Alan on the stairs. 'Shepherd's pie's in the oven,' he said.

'Great.' Alan didn't look back.

Spooky was holding a hip flask.

'Little early, for that, isn't it?' Alan said as he laid the mackerel on the chopping board.

'The depot at Penzance radioed,' Spooky said, ignoring the comment. 'The relief keeper's ill. I'm stuck here for another two days.' He took a gulp from the flask. Alan didn't like Spooky enough to feel sorry for him, but he didn't welcome an extra two days cooped up with him either. The scheduled relief was a mate of Alan's: Matt Bryant. Matt and Alan had worked together on Eddystone and Nab Tower. Matt was amiable and down-to-earth; they were cut from the same cloth. Alan took a knife from the block and sliced into the mackerel opening it along its spine.

'You don't like me very much, do you?' Spooky said as he placed a filter on a Rizla paper and gathered a line of tobacco behind it. Something told Alan Spooky was playing with him.

'Why do you say that?' Alan removed the belly fat with a quick, clean stroke.

'You hardly say two words to me from one end of the day to the other.'

'I'm not the talkative type.' Alan discarded the guts then he flipped the fish over and cut along the other side of the spine.

'You seem to get on all right with the newbie,' Spooky said.

Alan made two incisions on either side of the spine and pulled out the bone.

'Yeah,' Spooky continued. 'Looks like you've got a real cosy Papa Bear thing going on there.'

Alan turned and the knife blade caught the light and he said, 'What's that supposed to mean?'

'Calm down for Chrissakes.' Spooky said.

Alan let out a lengthy sigh and returned to gutting the fish. 'I'm sorry,' he said. 'I'm just a little tightly wound. The concussion, maybe.'

'Oh fuck it. Now I've dropped my bloody stuff.' Spooky knelt down and collected up the tobacco, and the paper and filter, and headed onto the stairs. 'I'm going out for a peaceful smoke then I'll be taking a nap. Tell Baby Bear to save my pie for later.'

Alan slammed the knife into the chopping board. Condensation dribbled gently down the walls. He opened the window then picked up a bream and dropped it onto the cutting board, slicing easily into the soft, white flesh.

iii

Jabe was cleaning the prisms with a damp chamois leather. The late morning sky had turned a grubby grey now and all over the sea white foam was breaking as far the horizon. Jabe's back ached. He stopped for a break, scratching the skin on his upper arm absent-mindedly. He was frustrated and more alone than ever. He had to get out of the optic suddenly, out into the open. He stepped out onto the gallery where the air was cool and brisk.

The morning watch would be over soon and he was looking forward to getting some sleep. Alan would take the afternoon watch and then Jabe would be back on 8pm till midnight. He leaned over the railing and saw Spooky marching purposefully away from the tower along the higher ground towards the north side of the rock. Jabe used to be glad when it was just him and Alan for lunch. Now that had changed. It occurred to him Devil's Rock lighthouse was becoming more and more like a silent order.

Alan was bagging up the fish for the deep freeze. They nodded to each other as Alan eased past and headed down to the freezer. Jabe set the table for two. Alan returned as he was spooning the pie onto plates. Time to bite the bullet. 'Listen,' Jabe said, not looking at him. 'Are we okay? We've not spoken to each other properly for days...'

'Yeah, we're good.'

'Are you sure about that?'

Alan put down his fork and raised his hand in a mollifying gesture. 'We're fine, really.'

'If you say so.'

'Look son, what happened - I've never done anything like that before.'

'And you don't want to do it again?'

'No, I don't. Try not to make a big deal out of it.'

'You're the one giving me the cold shoulder.'

'It's difficult for me. I can't let it go anywhere. I've got a wife, kids, a normal life.'

'I'm normal, Alan.'

'You know what I mean.'

'Yeah, I know exactly what you mean.'

'Look, kid. I'm not queer. And we've got a job to do.'

'So let's just get on with it.' Humiliation was stinging in Jabe's eyes. It took all his effort to face his feelings down. Bury them. Alan had made his choice: his wife, his kids, not Jabe. He had said it himself: he was not 'queer'. He lived in a different world entirely, a world he was happy to be part of.

iv

The tiny cafe was empty except for Laila in acid-wash jeans and an oversized purple jumper. She looked out at the unremarkable high street. All the usual suspects: Athena, Woolworths, Blockbuster Video. A blue Datsun Cherry parked on double yellows. The driver pulled on a baseball jacket, pocketed his aviators, and hurried into the newsagent. Moments later he came back carrying cigarettes and a packet of Polos. The waitress slapped a tuna jacket on the glass table in front of Laila then headed back behind the till to stare blankly out at the high street like a lookout in a crow's nest. She sighed theatrically when the bell jingled above the door and an old woman came in.

'Lola Beedie?' the woman asked Laila, pulling off her trench coat.

'Laila Bedi.'

'Apologies! I'm terrible with names.'

'Thank you for meeting me, Mrs Christie.'

'Miss.' The woman waved away Laila's apology before it left her lips. 'Why are you so eager to talk to an old author who specialises in the unexplained? And please, call me Ruth.'

'Can I get you anything, Ruth?'

'Coffee with cream quickens the senses, I always find.'

Once the waitress had taken the order, Laila told Ruth why she was trying to find out about the Slaying at Devil's Rock.

'That's very interesting,' Ruth took a sip of her coffee and raised an eyebrow. 'Mmm. Not at all bad! Since you contacted me, I've been going back through my notes. There were a couple of things I uncovered after the book had gone to print.' Ruth leaned forward confidentially, her ankh pendant almost dipping in her coffee. 'Of course, I just put it all in a box file and continued working on the next book.' She took another sip. 'I never quite understood why those poor men on Devil's Rock had their eyes gouged out. Then I was contacted by a chap up in

Edinburgh who'd read my book. Barney McFadden? Benny McFadden? Something like that. He fancied himself as a bit of a ghost hunter. He believed there was a connection between the murders on Devil's Rock and an Edinburgh serial killer called Walter Rickets, also known as the Beast of Southside. Walter's modus operandi was to gouge out his victims' eyes. Something to do with feelings of shame at what he'd done. When I looked at the newspaper reports from that time and did a little more digging at Somerset House, I discovered that one of the murdered keepers, Paul Roddick, had changed his name from Paul Rickets. It turned out Walter Rickets was his brother. Walter liked to keep certain mementoes from his victims: necklaces, rings, things of that sort. Some of these were engraved and could be traced back to the owners. The two brothers shared some pokey little rooms over a shop. It was Paul who found Walter's nasty little stash and called the police. When it all went to court, it was Paul's testimony that convicted Walter. Straight after the trial, Paul changed his name and went to work as a lighthouse keeper. Obviously he wanted to get as far away from his brother and the scandal as possible.'

Laila put her mug down on the smeared glass table. 'So that explains it,' she said. 'Walter Rickets came after his brother. He got onto the lighthouse and killed all three keepers.'

'Oh no, dear.' Ruth smiled sympathetically. 'This is where it gets really interesting. You see, there's absolutely no way Walter Rickets could have done it. Walter was hung for his crimes on the 15th of October 1861. Exactly one year before the Slaying took place. When those three keepers were murdered, Walter Rickets was already dead.'

Spooky said matter-of-factly:
'We can use the ouija to speak to the dead.'

chapter nine

i

Thursday 15th October 1987

The newsreader finished speaking. Ruth fidgeted in her chair, unable to settle, her lips pressed together in a tight thin line. The feeling that something terrible was going to happen had been building steadily all day. Now the weather forecaster appeared in bleary black and white: balding with a moustache and oversized wire-rimmed spectacles as far as she could tell (her Ferguson Courier portable never did get the best picture). He stood in front of a map of the British Isles which showed enormous banks of low pressure hanging over southeast England: *Good afternoon to you. Earlier on today a woman rang the BBC and said she heard there was a hurricane on the way. Well, if you're watching, don't worry. There isn't. But having said that, actually, the weather will become very windy. But most of the strong winds, incidentally, will be down over Spain and across into France as well. But there's a vicious-looking area of low pressure on our doorstep, nevertheless, around the Brittany area, and this is going to head across the southeastern corner of the country, bringing, if nothing else, a lot of rain with it.*

Ruth turned off the set and shook her head. The woman was not wrong. Ruth felt it. A huge storm was approaching. It was the same on the night of the 15th of October 1862, the night of the Slaying. She went into the study, moved the table out of the way and sat down on the olive green carpet (she'd been meaning to get it changed for years). She'd been meaning to get the whole place redecorated but there was always something far more interesting to do; track down a first edition on occultism or interview an eye witness. Now she had settled into the lotus position and began to concentrate. She had to be strong. She had to be prepared. She wasn't sure exactly what was going to happen later that night: she only knew it would be violent. Something unholy was growing in strength by the hour. She was right to insist the girl came down to see her.

Laila had taken the afternoon off - anything to get out of copy proofing. The night before, there had been a family get-together for her mother's birthday - wall-to-wall aunts, uncles, cousins, nieces and nephews, and the endless questions about whether she was seeing 'a boy'. Now she was cursing Ruth. Reading seemed like an interminable distance from London and the traffic on the M4 had slowed to a crawl. Why meet in person? Maybe Ruth was just a lonely old fruit cake. *Pump up the Volume* thundered out of the radio as she turned onto London Road then took a left onto De Beauvoir.

The street was narrow and long, lined with cars on either side and the houses stood tightly packed with broad Victorian bay windows. Laila edged her Austin Metro into the only free space. Rain pattered on her umbrella as she scanned the street to get her bearings. Number fifty-two was on the opposite side.

The small living room hadn't been decorated since the nineteen-fifties. Two well-worn sofas, one orange, one green, faced each other across a Melamine coffee table. A bronzed drinks trolley, loaded with spirits and an assortment of odd tumblers, stood next to a modest fireplace of mottled beige tiles. The walls were papered with green checks sprinkled with flowers. Ruth carried in a tray with a teapot, cups and a box of Crawford's Rover biscuits. She was wearing an outlandish paisley kaftan and a chiffon scarf around her head. She filled two cups. 'Lavender tea, my dear. Good for the soul. As is a nice biscuit.' She bit heartily into a bourbon cream and offered Laila the box.

'It's great to see you again so soon, Ruth,' Laila said. 'But why couldn't we just talk on the phone?'

'Because what I've discovered,' Ruth said, 'is too disturbing to discuss over the phone.' She sat forward, elbows on her knees. 'I stopped off at the British Library.' She clapped her hands together and bobbed up and down in her chair like a child. 'I found an obscure reference by a chap called P. R. Frobisher. Very plodding writer - dull as dishwater - but what he had to say about Devil's Rock was thrilling. He'd uncovered a little-known incident in the 18th Century involving a group of Franciscan monks.

They were passengers on the Amsterdam, a Dutch fluyt sailing to the Americas in 1737. On the night of the 15th of October, the seas were heavy and driving the ship towards Devil's Rock. One of the brothers fell badly and broke his neck, and was killed instantly. The other monks wrapped his body in a blanket. As the crew struggled to regain control of the ship, a mass of water between the Amsterdam and the rock started moving strangely.

'The ship was dragged closer and closer to the rock and a dreadful cold overtook the deck, seeping into every plank and beam, every bend and curve. Then a dim light appeared above the moving water and, just as abruptly, vanished. Moments later the dead monk came to life, roaring like a maniac, attacking the poor sailors and throwing them into the roiling sea. The deckhands tried to overpower him but he had the strength of twenty men. Eventually, one of them managed to strike him hard from behind and he fell overboard and was swept away. The water stopped moving oddly and the ship was saved. After the events of that night, the monks concluded that the water marked one of Satan's gateways into hell.'

Laila realised she was gripping the soles of her shoes with her toes. 'That is very, very creepy,' she said, 'but it was centuries ago. What has it got to do with Devil's Rock now?'

'Think about it my dear,' said Ruth. 'From what your lighthouse keeper friend says, there are 'unusual' things happening on Devil's Rock right now.'

'How are they connected?'

'The dates: 1737, 1862, 1987 - spaced exactly one hundred and twenty-five years apart.'

'Coincidence.'

'No, I don't think so.' Ruth scanned Laila's face. She couldn't remember the last time she'd felt so certain. 'There's also the question of the day. Both grisly events took place on the 15th of October. Today's date. If anything is going to happen on Devil's Rock, it's going to happen tonight.'

'Let's say there is a pattern: 15th of October, one hundred and twenty years.'

'One hundred and twenty-five years.'

'Right, but those things happened during terrible storms. There's no storm now.'

'It's on its way, dear. There was talk of a hurricane on the weather report this afternoon.'

'That was just some crazy. Michael Fish laughed.'

'But he's wrong and she's right. I'm 'a sensitive'. I was born with the gift. Your friend on the lighthouse is in danger. All those men are in danger. I suggest we contact those who have gone before us: the men who were murdered in the Slaying.'

ii

Spooky stabbed a sliver of pepper with his fork and wagged it at Jabe. 'There's no bloody hurricane coming, newbie. Just some rough weather is all.'

'They were talking about a hurricane on the TV,' Jabe said. 'The wind's furious outside.'

'You'll have to get used to it or maybe you're just not cut out for being a keeper?'

'Or maybe you should just button it?' Alan said flatly.

'Daddy to the rescue,' Spooky smirked. Alan's anger was clear and bright for a moment before he managed to hold himself in check. 'Weren't we supposed to be tucking into some nice juicy mackerel,' Spooky said, 'not eating bloody vegetable pasta?'

Jabe flushed. 'I forgot to get it out of the freezer.'

'Ignore him kid,' Alan said. 'He's just got the hump because he's stuck here with us for an extra couple of days.'

iii

The wind was wrathful, the waves cresting to thirty feet. The tower flung out its beam over the water, a thin thread of light in the bitter wreck of a night.

'Old Bill Norton would have whipped the newbie into shape,' Spooky muttered to himself, tapping his forefinger on the table. 'Cantankerous old bastard. His missus must be glad he's gone.'

'How can you say that?' Jabe said.

'You didn't know him. He was a hard man to love.' Spooky said.

'Difficult to imagine what really happened.' Alan said.

'Why don't we ask him?' Spooky said. He disappeared for a couple of minutes and Jabe and Alan looked at each other uncomfortably.

'The more time I spend with this guy, the madder I think he is.' Alan said.

They had secured the tower's storm shutters against the weather but the noise of the wind was terrific. Jabe hadn't slept well the last couple of nights. The 15th of October was never a good time. His father's death on the eve of his birthday made all birthdays impossible. He hadn't mentioned the date to Alan or Spooky. He couldn't bring himself to. He felt a queasy vibration as the tower moved under the weight of the sea. His ears popped. He scratched nervously at his left arm.

'You'll make it bleed,' Alan said.

Spooky came back with a dusty cardboard box. He took out a wooden board with the words 'yes' and 'no', the letters of the alphabet, and the numbers zero to nine. Spooky said matter-of-factly: 'We can use the ouija to speak to the dead.'

iv

Ruth was sitting with her head slightly tilted, as if listening intently for something. She took Laila's hands carefully in her own. The room was cool but Ruth was fiercely hot to the touch even though there wasn't a trace of perspiration on her.

'When I have made contact,' Ruth said. 'The spirits will speak through me. You will need to ask them questions.'

Laila looked unsure.

'You will know what to say when the moment arrives.' Ruth closed her eyes and began to inhale and exhale deeply. Gradually her breathing steadied and slowed. 'I want you to concentrate on your friend. Think of him and the danger he faces tonight on Devil's Rock.'

Laila didn't like how that sounded. She swallowed hard and her throat made a little clicking noise. She pictured Jabe standing in her kitchen. It was the day before his interview at Trinity House. He had been so keen / she had felt he was just running away. He had seemed optimistic / she thought maybe he would always be running away. Her thoughts were interrupted by Ruth's grip, now fierce and terrifically cold. The cold colonised Laila's body, running up her arms, flowering in her chest.

Then Ruth's head drooped forwards.

'There is a presence.' She stiffens. Her head snaps upright. She is gripping Laila's fingers so tightly, she might break them. Her breath is rasping and very fast. Her voice is a man's voice and it is harsh and resentful. 'Who are you?' it says to Laila, 'Why have you brought me here?'

For a brief moment Laila can't speak. 'I want to know about Devil's Rock,' she stutters.

The answering laugh is low, guttural. 'Devil's Rock is the gateway between worlds. An ingress for evil and sickness drawn into your world by the nexus.'

'What's the nexus?'

'The nexus is the link, the trigger. There must always be a nexus.'

Laila's heart pounds against the unnatural cold in her chest. 'Is my friend in danger? Is Jabe in danger?'

Ruth's grin is foul. She lifts her head, 'The storm is come. The waters rise, the gate opens. There is nothing you can do for any soul on Devil's Rock.'

'Who are you?' Laila whispers. 'How do you know all this?'

Ruth's eyelids flick open. Only milky whiteness shows because her eyes have rolled up in their sockets. 'Don't you know me, little girl?' Ruth's lips draw back wetly from her teeth. 'I am Walter Rickets.' She stands up suddenly and the coffee table clatters into the fireplace as she stabs and claws at Laila's eyes.

The air is ringing with the dead clang of metal. Alan leads the way down the last few steps to the entrance to the tower.

chapter ten

i

Ruth's nails land like razor wire just short of their target. Laila kicks and thrashes in her attempt to get away. She grabs Ruth's wrists and tries to push her onto the floor but now the old woman has the strength of a prize fighter. They fall and land in a heap by the hearth. Ruth forces Laila onto her back. Blood is welling up in red pips across Laila's neck. Laila slaps the old woman across the face as hard as she can and Ruth lets out a low moan, and lurches onto her side. Laila grabs the fire poker and raises it defensively like a sword. All of sudden, she is Jean d'Arc, righteous in the light of God. Ruth is completely still before the French saint. Still as a corpse. Still. Laila/Jean d'Arc turns her over gingerly and, slowly, Ruth opens her eyes, winces.

101

'Good grief,' she groaned, raising herself up on one elbow. 'What on earth happened to you?'

'You went crazy,' Laila said. 'You were babbling about being Walter Rickets. You tried to gouge my eye out.'

'Oh, how awful, how utterly dreadful. Rickets was acting through me, of course, using me as a vessel. I don't remember a bit of it but here you are, shivering with the shock. Let me get you a blanket and a hot drink.' She rubbed the side of her head. 'Did you hit me? Jolly good show, dear.'

'Are you ok?'

'Used to be captain of the hockey team in my youth. Took a mighty knock on the chin once - didn't bat an eyelid. You broke Rickets' hold over me: that's the important thing. We have to help those poor men on Devil's Rock. They really are in the most terrible danger.'

'I'm sorry I doubted.' Laila said. 'Rickets is a monster.'

'Not Rickets. He's gone. He was just the John-the-Baptist for something far worse.' Ruth retrieved a woollen blanket from her bedroom and wrapped it gently round Laila's shoulders. 'The spirits often communicate through me but there's never been any physical violence before.'

Laila watched the old woman pour hot milk into a mug and add a generous spoonful of honey.

'Drink this while it's hot and we'll bathe those scratches and then we can talk about what we're going to do. I am so sorry about hurting you.'

Ruth bathed Laila's wounds in warm salty water. 'I think we must go down to Cornwall and see if we can't get over to Devil's Rock somehow under our own steam.'

'But if there's a storm coming we'll never get there.'

'My feeling is that we just need to be close. The closer

I am, the easier it will be to understand what they're up against and to help them in some way.'

'Perhaps I should go by myself,' Laila said.

'I won't hear of it and, anyway, one of us will have to navigate. I used to be a Brown Owl. Always prepared.'

Laila looked doubtful.

'Don't worry. Rickets is completely gone. There won't be any more incidents like that between us again, I promise.'

'It's a long way down to Cornwall, Ruth.'

'I'm not an invalid. When I was your age, I was dodging doodlebugs and German bombers. I'm sixty-seven and ready for anything!' No matter how much Laila tried to dissuade her, Ruth wouldn't be denied. She disappeared to find a flask and brew some strong coffee. It was going to be a long night.

ii

'No way,' Alan said, looking at the ouija board.'

'I want to do it,' Jabe said simply.

Alan glanced at him, wide-eyed. Even Spooky seemed a little surprised. Jabe carried on, 'There's something not right: Bill Norton dying, Alan's accident.'

'They're just things that happen on a rock station,' Alan said.

'I really want to do this.' Jabe's voice was oddly tight. 'Something's really not right. Up in the lantern, I heard someone speaking.'

'The wind,' Alan offered.

'No.' Jabe insisted. 'And I saw the shadow of someone.'

Alan thought the boy must be losing it like the other

kid, Vinnie Wells.

'The ouija board works better if there are more of us,' Spooky said. 'Not so good with just two.'

A few seconds passed but it seemed longer.

'All right,' Alan said quietly. He could see what was happening: the boy's first time on a rock station, his imagination running away with him. Best lay 'the ghosts' to rest.

'This is the planchette,' Spooky showed them a small heart-shaped block of wood on castors. 'You put your fingers on top, like this.'

Alan stared down at the board. He knew exactly how a seance worked: a Saturday night in late autumn some twenty odd years ago. His parents out. His sister Laura and her fiancée Tom were minding him. He remembered Laura coaxing him gently, telling him there was no harm in it. Nothing to be frightened of. He was eleven years old. He watched as Laura and Tom laid out some crudely cut pieces of paper, a letter scribbled on each. They upended a sherry glass and each of them placed a finger on the base. Laura asked if there was anybody else in the room with them. Alan shivered in spite of himself. Tom ribbed him about being girly, being a scaredy cat. The glass moved slowly from letter to letter. A child had died, hit by a car, not killed outright but dying slowly, and in terrible pain. She said she was cold and frightened and alone, and trapped in darkness. Laura snatched her hand away from the glass. The contact was broken. Playing with the dead wasn't so amusing suddenly. Tom told her not to be so bloody daft. It was just a bit of nonsense. He admitted to pushing the glass. They quarrelled. Laura was shouting. Tom was standing square, arms folded, eyes like a firestorm. It was the last fight before they broke up. Alan went up and hid away in his room. He'd been taken in, humiliated so easily by a cheap trick.

Jabe rested his fingertips on the planchette. His mouth was dry. Devil's Rock had found its way into his blood. He was at the edge of something, about to fall. Spooky looked straight ahead. 'Everybody concentrate.'

A pattern appeared a little way from Devil's Rock on the spiking surface of the sea. Something was moving oddly in the deep, funnelling up columns of salt water.

'We call upon any spirit present,' Spooky said. 'Is anybody there?'

The water was moving slowly but methodically. The surface was breaking up, needles of water, rising and falling. Something was waiting for its moment, hardened and brilliant with hatred.

'Is anybody there?'

Now the thing crosses the bridge between worlds. Now it moves towards the tower, towards the boy, the nexus.

'Is anybody there?'

Alan smiled to himself. It was like an old Boris Karloff film. He didn't notice the room growing colder or the condensation slowing and thickening on the walls. He stopped smiling as the planchette slid smoothly across the board to the word 'YES'.

'Who are you?' Spooky said. The planchette moved from letter to letter: I-W-I-L-L-K-I-L-L. Jabe was suddenly lightheaded.

'Kill?' Spooky said. 'Who will you kill?'

A-L-L.

'All? Everybody... everybody here?'

YES.

'Why?'

Again, the planchette moved: B-I-T-C-H.

'What do you mean?'

L-I-T-T-L-E-B-I-T-C-H-L-I-T-T-L-E-T-W-I-G-G-Y…

Jabe throws the planchette across the table. He sees his father's face blunt with rage. He sees his mother's injured head. He sees the blood on his hands. Then the lights go out.

Jabe holds his fingers up in front of his face and sees nothing.

'What the fuck,' he hears Spooky curse.

Then Alan's voice: 'Are you okay?'

'No.'

'Listen,' Spooky says. 'The generator's stopped.' Only the rushing of the sea outside, only the wind, only the endless pattering and re-pattering sea.

Alan's voice again: 'The power will be out for the whole tower. The light! Does anyone have a match?'

Spooky: 'In my pocket. Hang on.'

The little flame lights the space above the table a sickly yellow.

'Over here,' Alan beckons to Spooky. They try to switch on the battery light, but it's dead. 'Christ! What the hell's going on? We need to get the storm shutters open. We'll have to risk a breach.' They stumble to the window and push the shutters back. Moonlight filters dimly into the room and Jabe is able to make out the sink top, the TV set, the oven. Alan finds torches; tosses one to Spooky. The beams play across the furniture, dance over foolscap folders, VHS tapes, tins of food and they are belongings

106

abandoned on a sinking ship.

'Something bad is going down.' Spooky says in a high-pitched voice. 'What the fuck? Something really fucking bad is going down.'

'Shut up!' Alan's voice is very loud in the tight space of the room. Then a single cacophonous bang echoes up from the base of the tower. Then it sounds again; something banging on metal. Then it sounds again.

'What the hell is it?' Jabe whispers.

'Something's at the doors,' Spooky croaks. 'Jesus Christ. The thing from the ouija. It's going to get in. It's going to kill us.'

Alan reaches him in a stride: 'Shut up and get a bloody grip. You're the acting PK.'

'You can have the bloody job.'

Alan looks at Jabe. 'You and Cyrus go up top and check on C engine,' he says. 'Find out what the problem is. Try and get it started. I'll go down and find out what the noise is.' He goes out onto the stairs.

Jabe follows him. 'I should go with you,' he says. Truth is, he feels safer with Alan.

Alan calls back to Spooky impatiently, 'Go and check the generator!' He is struggling to keep his voice even. 'There's no light, we're showing no light. Get the generator going again.'

Spooky picks up his torch and heads upstairs.

The storm shutters on the lower floors are braced closed. The darkness is absolute. The steps are narrower than usual. The air is thick as glue. Dead engines produce no steady rhythm to compete with the sound of the sea. Alan and Jabe open the storm shutters level by level until they reach the winch room. Jabe sees the winch as a giant

107

red dragon. The winch chains are grotesque torture apparatus. By the base of the tower, the banging is unbelievably loud. The air is ringing with the dead clang of metal. Alan leads the way down the last few steps to the entrance to the tower. As far as he can see, the doors are secure. No water. No breach.

'Take the light and get behind me,' Alan says. The onslaught from the outside is incessant now. Whatever's on the other side knows they're there.

'What do you think it is?' Jabe says.

'It's not water, that's for sure.'

Jabe is back in a childhood nightmare: the goblin is under the bed, the wolf man is on the landing, branches are scratching at the window, things are going bump in the night. Alan hits the underside of the first bracing bar, now the second, and starts to open the doors. But he is knocked to the ground by something very large. Jabe drops the torch. Everything turns black.

The writhing thing doesn't seem to hear. It seems in intolerable pain, foaming at the mouth, fitting.

chapter eleven

i

The passageway rages with unhuman staccato sounds. Jabe searches for the torch by touch, then the beam is skittering across the stairway, catching Alan's face and his hands beating like paddles. Something is twisting on the floor. It is in the shape of a man, only different in some way. Jabe is very afraid of the thing on the floor. He is shouting and the light from the torch is swinging around insanely.

'Keep the light steady!' Alan is shouting. 'I'll turn him over.' Alan is leaning over the struggling thing. For a second a head appears in the beam, mottled and purplish. The eyes are blank. The eyelids are waxy and swollen. The thing is soaking wet and thrashing about like a suffocating eel. Now a roller is curling in through the open doors, sweeping Alan and Jabe and the struggling thing down the passage to the foot of the stairs.

'Shut the doors!' Alan calls out as he tries to hold on to the huge form. 'It's all right. Listen to me, you're going to be all right.' The writhing thing doesn't seem to hear. It seems in intolerable pain, foaming at the mouth, fitting.

'I said shut the fucking doors!' Alan's voice jolts Jabe back to reality. He reaches the storm doors as another wave curls into the tower. He is slipping and stumbling and falling against the doors, and shouldering them shut and ramming the bars into position just as another wave hits.

'Go ahead of me,' Alan said. 'Light the way.' Jabe was trembling, doing his best to keep the torch steady. The light jerked and flickered over dripping pipework, storage crates and the stairs running with water. He lost his footing, recovered his balance. Alan was close behind, half-carrying, half-dragging the dark thing up the stairs. It fought him all the way. Alan dropped him and struggled to get him upright again. The veins were standing out like cords on Alan's neck.

'I'd better help you.' Jabe said.

'Just hold the light steady.' Alan heaved the man onto the landing, struggling to catch his breath. 'Christ, he weighs a fucking ton.'

Then the un-man broke away somehow, worming strangely across the constricted space, almost knocking Jabe back down the stairs. Alan seized hold of the massive bulk and, with one last almighty effort, hauled it into the sleeping quarters. They got it onto a bunk but it was still moving strangely and drooling from the mouth. 'We'll have to restrain it or it'll hurt itself – or us. Get the boat rope as quickly as you can.' Alan said.

Spooky appeared at the door. 'It's no good. C engine is dead.' Then he saw the form on the bed, 'Jesus Christ,' he said, 'Bill Norton!'

Norton hisses. His pupils are black discs. He tries to reach for Spooky but Alan holds him fast on the bunk. 'Jabe, where's that bloody rope?'

Alan binds Norton's wrists and feet. Spooky's face is incredibly pale: 'Jesus, he looks like some kind of fucking zombie. A walking dead man. And he smells bad.'

'Are you sure that's him?' Alan asks.

'That's Bill Norton, all right.'

'But how can it be?' Jabe says. 'He was lost at sea.'

'There's got to be an explanation,' says Alan.

It seems obvious to Spooky: 'Something came in through the ouija, and brought him back with it.'

'That's enough!' Alan snaps. 'We need to work out what to do next. Have you checked the other engines?'

'Not yet.'

'See what you can do with A and B engines. Otherwise it'll have to be the station batteries. We must get the light running again. I'll contact the depot.'

Alan tried the UHF phone. It was dead. He tried the coastguard on the RT phone. Dead again. He slammed a fist onto the desk top.

'This can't be happening,' Jabe said in a whisper. 'Why is nothing working?'

'How the hell do I know?' Jabe flinched and Alan shifted awkwardly, rubbing his neck with the palm of his hand. 'Sorry, mate. We've just got to deal with things as best we can, okay?' He took Jabe's chin between thumb and forefinger and Jabe returned a colourless smile. 'It'll be all right, kid, I promise. The guys on the Wolf will see our light's out.'

'What if their power's out too?'

'Then mainland will work it out when we don't report in.' Alan saw the fright on Jabe's face. 'I don't pretend to know what's going on, but we've got to focus on getting the light back on for the ships out there.'

The moon glimmered sickly. It said they were too alone, too far out in the middle of the sea. They were the crew of a scuttled submarine.

'A and B are dead, and so are the batteries,' Spooky said.

'Shit,' Alan couldn't believe what he was hearing. 'No luck with the UHF either.'

'Then we're completely cut off,' said Spooky. 'Something's deliberately shutting us off from the outside world. We've disturbed something. And now it wants us.'

'Listen, mate,' Alan said. 'I don't know what's knocked out all the power but it sure as hell wasn't Count Dracula.'

'If the station batteries aren't working,' said Jabe. 'How come the torches are still working?'

'It's toying with us,' said Spooky. 'It's going to pick us off one by one.'

'Will you just fucking pack it in?' Alan told him.

'I need a drink.'

'No you don't. We all need to keep our heads clear. We've got to get light to the top of the tower.'

'Do we have any candles?' Jabe asked. 'If we put them inside the optic, we'd be showing some kind of light at least.'

'There are some old oil lamps down next to the freezer.'

114

Spooky said.

'That'll do it.' Alan said. He tossed his torch to Jabe. 'You go and check on our guest.'

The night terrors always find a way in. The bogeymen, the monsters, the greys, the rippers are always just behind the bedroom door. The sea is full of monsters. The conger eel moves in the inky water and opens its razor-sharp jaws wide. The tower is full of nightmares. The air is sour and cold. All around, the ocean is in colossal turmoil, massing to overwhelm the little spire of Devil's Rock lighthouse.

ii

Jabe presses his ear to the door of the bunk room. Silence. He pushes gently at the door and it squeaks queasily as it opens. Everything is wrong. Bill Norton lies flat and still, head turned to the wall. Jabe hears his own boots squeaking against the floor. He moves closer. Squeak. Squeak. A little closer still. Squeak. Squeak. He is at the bed. He doesn't shine his torch directly at the bunk for fear of driving Norton crazy.

'Mr Norton? Bill?' he whispers. 'Are you okay?' He reaches out to touch the motionless form. Its skin is rotting and foul-smelling. 'Mr Norton?' Norton's head pivots on its neck. The eyes are soulless and obsidian. He bites Jabe's hand, breaking the barrier of skin, finding warm blood. Jabe yelps and cowers back like an injured dog. Norton hisses. Norton rasps. Norton blows. Norton speaks: 'I'll snap your bones. Little Twiggy. Little bitch.'

'The Exorcist was a real-life case. The Devil possessed a boy called Robbie Mannheim.'

[faint mirrored text from previous page, illegible]

chapter twelve

i

Grimy cloud low over the city. Drizzle fretting London's streets. Cars with their sidelights on in the middle of the day. Jabe's mother takes him to Hamleys to choose a Christmas present. He knows exactly what he wants. He reaches up to the shelf with the beautiful Barbies. His mother is horribly uncomfortable. Of course he can have the doll, but let's look at the Action Men or Planet of the Apes figures first. He does, happily enough. But he keeps coming back to the lovely Barbies. With a fixed smile, she takes a Barbie to the till and tells the assistant it's for her niece. She breaks the budget by buying the board game 'Mastermind' as well. Jabe is to show Mastermind to his father and hide Barbie under his bed.

He is fascinated by the little kitten-heeled shoes that

slot onto Barbie's tiny feet. He is fascinated by her large, painted eyes, by her perfect red lips. When the doll's clothes wear out, his mother tries to do the right thing and makes a new dress for Barbie. His father comes home early from work. The doll is lying on the kitchen table. Rufus Walker guesses immediately what's going on with his embarrassment of a son.

He is shouting obscenities at Jabe's mother. He knocks her out of the way. He is coming for Jabe. He smacks him around the head, throws him over his knee, pulls down his trousers and underpants and beats him. Then he tries to force the doll into Jabe's mouth. *'Eat this, you little bitch. Fucking little Twiggy.'* He holds Barbie in front of Jabe and snaps off her lovely arms and her long, slender, shapely legs. *'If I catch you playing with dolls again, I'll snap your bones. Little Twiggy. Little bitch.'*

ii

Norton's bite marks were livid under the cold water tap. What if Norton had infected him with something? Jabe dried his hand quickly and pulled down his sleeve.

Alan appeared at the door, carrying a cardboard box. 'We've put a load of block candles up in the optic,' he said. 'Tried to turn it manually but the handle won't budge. At least now it will be giving out some kind of light. I've brought the oil lamps.' He took two candles from the box, put them on the table and lit them. Then he took out six oil lamps and set them in a row. He removed the chimneys and burners and Jabe helped him fill the chambers with kerosene. Once they replaced the wicks and chimneys, it would be at least another hour before the wicks had soaked up the fuel and the lamps were ready to use.

'Where's Cyrus?' Jabe asked.

'Gone to see if we have more paraffin in the stores. And probably to get that bloody hip flask of his.'

Jabe shifted his weight a little guiltily.

'How was Norton?' Alan asked.

'He bit me.' Jabe held up his wounded hand.

'Jesus Christ! Alan came close, turning Jabe's hand over in his.

'Alan, he said things.'

'He spoke to you?'

'Yeah, he said things no one else could know.'

'I don't follow.'

Jabe wasn't sure how to put it.

'My dad…' Jabe's expression was intent and strained. 'I wasn't enough of a boy for him. He used to call me names. His favourite was Twiggy. He thought I was too skinny, like a girl. He also called me a little bitch. Norton said the same words just now.'

'Any chance he knew your dad?'

'My dad died when I was ten.'

'What happened?'

'I killed him.'

Alan pressed his hand to his head, wrong-footed for a moment.

'He used to beat me. He beat my mum too.' Jabe said. 'One day she tried to stop him. I thought he was going to kill her. So I killed him first.'

Alan sat down slowly.

'What if some part of my dad got inside Norton?'

Alan looked at him squarely. 'That's not possible.'

'But what if it is?'

119

'You're just scared.' Alan told him firmly. He put his arms around Jabe and pressed his lips lightly against his temple. 'I won't let anything bad happen. We'll get through this.'

iii

Norton is bellowing at the top of his lungs. The noise is wild, out of control.

'Fuck me!' Spooky is standing at the door. 'What the hell's got into him?' Jabe and Alan move quickly apart. They have no idea how long Spooky has been standing there.

'He must have lost his mind,' Alan says, clearing his throat. 'Out in the sea all that time.'

'It's not a normal man up there, pal.'

'You've been watching too many Hammer horrors.'

'We just have to sit tight until they come to check on us,' Spooky said, 'and hope the Evil Dead upstairs doesn't get loose.'

'A stiff drink might help,' said Jabe.

'Medicinal purposes?' Spooky's eyes lit up.

'Okay, medicinal purposes!' Alan agreed.

'I need something after what Norton said.'

'What did Norton say?' asked Spooky.

'Don't…' Alan cautioned Jabe.

'No. I want to talk about it.'

Norton is howling like a banshee in the room above their heads.

Spooky moved towards Jabe. 'What did he say to you?'

'He said he was going to kill us all.'

'Like the ouija.'

120

'Yes. And he said something else too. He called me things only my dead father could know.'

'This isn't doing any good.' Alan told him, folding his arms.

'Yes it is,' said Spooky. 'There's something controlling Norton.' He looked at Jabe. 'Could it be your father?'

'Oh Christ,' Alan said, 'you're both nuts.'

Spooky ignored him, turning back to Jabe. 'What did Norton say?'

'He called me a little bitch. Then he called me Twiggy. Things my dad used to say.'

'You're daddy's back, newbie.'

'Jesus,' Alan said. 'If you could only hear yourselves.'

'*The Exorcist* was a real-life case,' Spooky said. 'The Devil possessed a boy called Robbie Mannheim.'

'I did not know that,' Alan sighed, 'but what I do know is that there are plenty of gullible people who believe all sorts of –'

'Listen!' Jabe said. 'Norton's stopped howling.'

Norton is silent as the grave.

'He's probably worn himself out.'

'Has anyone checked to see if the Wolf's light is still showing?' Jabe asked. Alan went to the window: a flash at the horizon, fifteen seconds then another. 'Looks like everything's okay over there. They have to realise something's amiss with us any time now.'

'Unless they've still got their storm shutters closed.' Jabe said.

'I'd better go up and check the candles in the lantern,' Alan said.

Alan notices a strangeness in the atmosphere. The lantern room is filled with an unfamiliar sickly sweetness. He goes into the optic. He will feel better once they get the oil lamps lit, say two in the optic and the rest placed strategically up and down the tower to give as much light as possible. He knows he needs to keep Spooky quiet. The kid is jumpy enough.

He thinks about his own kids: uncommunicative and impossible to read, like all kids that age. He pictures the boys, and his wife, Debbie. He proposed when he was just eighteen. He wasn't desperate to settle down: tying the knot early was just what you did. His mother and father married as soon as they left school so he did the same. Debbie was dependable and devoted to the kids but a little too ready to nitpick after a couple of Pinot Grigios. When was he going to get round to the tongue and groove in the bathroom? Couldn't he spend less money down the pub and put more away for a holiday? Their house in Chelmsford was nice enough but increasingly cramped as the boys grew into men. Then there was the mortgage, the interminable mortgage.

Alan wonders what he is going to do when he is finally replaced by automation. Maybe Jabe is the lucky one. He's young enough to slot easily into another career. And, being the way he is, he'll escape the obligations of marriage and family - not that Alan doesn't love his wife and kids.

Occupied by these thoughts, he doesn't notice the dark thing moving in the lantern behind him. He doesn't notice the oddly un-human form until it is too late.

His torch cleaves the black: monitors, console dials and switches appear and pass in the torch's stuttering beam.

chapter thirteen

i

A deafening boom like a bomb going off. The living quarters illumined in splashes of vivid red. Spooky and Jabe shade their eyes against the glare. Jabe goes to the window. 'Someone's sent up a flare. There's a yacht,' he says, pointing, 'out on the northern spur.' Speared on an outcrop about five hundred yards north and tipped at a steep angle, a Snowgoose 37 lies with an angry gash in her side. The boat's port side is taking a vicious beating from the sea. It is lurching with drunken abandon on its spike of rock. Jabe can see two people gesticulating on the tilting deck.

'Fuck!' Spooky says.

'Let's go,' says Jabe. 'There are people out there. They need help.'

'Don't be a fool in this weather. No sense in putting

everyone in danger.'

Jabe grabs his waterproofs. The oddest feeling takes hold – that the tower itself is aware of him and laying out his destiny for him. He pulls on his sou'wester, turns up the collar of his oilskins and strides out onto the landing stage. The land itself is a kind of anger: the rocks rise up in angry peaks. The wind is furious. He moves carefully over the slick surface of the landing, clambers down onto the rocks, head down against the oncoming spray. The yacht comes back into view and he sees three people on deck. One of them jumps down onto the foaming rocks and reaches up to help the next.

Jabe continues northwards. Here the rocks jut out like so much spite thrown into the sea and the wind tears at his hair, punishes his cheeks and his hands. He has to cling to the rock to prevent himself being swept into the sea like an unloved doll. All three of the yacht's crew are now safely down on the rock and moving gingerly in his direction. Instinctively, he looks back towards the tower. The paralysed light from the optic seems piteously inadequate. He reaches a ridge of rising fists and fingers of rock and sees the yacht's crew on the other side: one man, two women.

'Follow me!' he shouts, gesturing towards the tower. The man raises a hand in acknowledgement then waves to the women to follow. They fight the wind and the sea and the treachery underfoot and reach the entrance of the tower. As Jabe puts his back against the doors to force them closed, he is able to get a better look at the new arrivals.

The man was slight, very pale skinned. Jabe guessed he was in his late forties. His eyebrows had been lifted and his cheeks tightened by surgery. His nose was strong, lips narrow and he had a thick shock of hair, dyed boot-polish black. He wore a diamond stud in his left ear. The younger of the two women had bleached hair, pale blue eyes and orange, tanning-booth skin. Jabe had a feeling he had seen her somewhere before. The older woman must have been in her mid-thirties but had a presence that made her seem older. She was of Caribbean heritage, tall and hefty in a way that added to her natural gravitas.

'Is everybody okay?' Jabe asked.

'Where was the bloody light?' the man replied.

'The power is out.'

'Leave it, Cooper.' It was the young white woman who spoke, resting a conciliatory hand on the man's arm. 'He's obviously the junior.'

The man was hot with anger. 'We ran aground because the fucking light wasn't showing.'

'The boat was out of control,' the black woman said in soft Welsh tones. 'We would have hit the rocks anyway.'

'Shut up. And it isn't 'a boat', it's a very expensive yacht.'

'Can we just go upstairs and get warm, please?' the white woman asked.

The older woman stepped forwards and offered Jabe her hand. 'I'm Brenda Rogers. This is Vanessa Riley. And this gentleman, in case you didn't know already, is Cooper Reid.' Jabe realised Vanessa Riley was a Page Three model: her topless calendar was above the Baby Belling in the living quarters. He didn't know who Cooper was, but Brenda and Cooper seemed to think he should.

'Jabe Walker. This way to the living quarters,' he said. 'It's not very warm I'm afraid because of the power.'

iii

They took off their life preservers and waterproof jackets. Jabe noticed they were still wet through - experienced sailors would have worn full waterproof gear in this kind of weather. Their faces were wraith-like in the candlelight. He noticed Brenda was wearing a chef's coat.

'Why don't you light these?' Cooper asked, nodding at the row of lamps on the table.

'The wicks have to soak up the fuel first.'

'When will the power be back on?'

'We don't know.'

'You must have emergency generators?'

'They're not working.'

Vanessa picked up the bottle on the table. 'Any glasses?'

'We're not in a frigging wine bar, love,' said Cooper. 'We've got bigger things to worry about than your self-medicating.' He looked at Jabe. 'I need to call the mainland. Can I use the ship-to-shore?'

'Nothing's working.'

'So we're completely cut off?'

'Yes.'

'Jesus H. Christ!'

'How long until they send someone out here to check on the lighthouse?' Brenda asked gently.

Before Jabe could reply, Cooper cut in: 'So let's get this right? Your captain, or whoever's in charge of this dump, has buggered up the power during a major storm? And now we're all stuck here. Frigging fantastic.'

128

'There's nothing we can do right now.'

'Not good enough, sunshine. You do know who I am?'

'I don't think he does,' Vanessa smirked, waving her hand towards the calendar on the wall. 'But you know who I am don't you darling?' Even though he'd never really looked at the calendar, Jabe still flushed crimson. 'Listen honey, let me put you out of your misery. This lovely man is THE Cooper Reid. Lead guitarist from Davey and the Shakers. They're a VERY old pop group from the Sixties. Never quite as famous as the Beatles or even Herman's Hermits.'

'Famous enough to keep you in fur coats and expensive yachts.' Cooper told her.

'Your expensive toy's a write-off, dearest.'

'Shut it.' Cooper scowled. 'Where's the chief, sunshine? The sooner I speak to someone in charge, the sooner I can get the hell out of here.'

'How do you propose to do that?' Brenda asked him. 'The skipper can't do anything with no power and no communications. You'll just have to wait here like the rest of us.'

'Stick to currying goats and making jambalaya. In fact, make yourself useful and go and rustle us up something now.'

'What part of 'there's no power' don't you understand?' Cooper was winding Brenda up tight.

'Drop the attitude, Rustie Lee, or I'll have you flipping burgers at Wimpy's by tomorrow morning.' Brenda gave him a defiant smile and looked out of the window.

'I thought you were going to get the boss, sunshine?' Cooper said.

129

Jabe can't find Alan or Spooky. When he reaches the sleeping quarters, he sees the door is ajar. He shines his torch in the direction of Norton's bunk, and the bunk is empty. The ropes that held Norton are broken, shredded. Jabe swings the light wildly, expecting Norton to appear behind him. Please God, let it have left the tower, Jabe thinks to himself. The stairs are whispering about a hundred hidden horrors. His torch cleaves the black: monitors, console dials and switches appear and pass in the torch's stuttering beam. The click and hum of machinery has been replaced absolutely now by the unholy protests of the sea. How easily the machine of the colossal tower has been silenced. How completely human beings have come to rely on technology and how lost they are when it fails. The tower and its technology are petrified, null things in the emphatic reality of the storm. Everyone on Devil's Rock is exposed and unprotected.

The door to the top engine room is closed. Jabe takes the red fire axe from the wall and grips it firmly. He eases the door open. The stairs on the other side are steeper than usual. And empty. He sees the dimmest light filtering down from the lantern. He feels a surge of relief. Alan is up there, making sure the candles are still burning, keeping an eye on things.

'Alan? Are you there?'

Silence.

'Alan?'

Something a little more than silence.

He climbs the stairs, axe in hand, alert for the slightest movement. The fog signal compressors appear like torpedo tubes, primed for death. He passes the dead station batteries and reaches the metal ladder leading up into the lantern itself.

'Alan!' Jabe calls again. 'If you're there, please answer me.'

Silence.

Jabe's palms are wet against the handle of the axe. He pockets the torch and grasps the first rung of the ladder. His eyes are trained on the gap above his head. He climbs. He reaches the top of the ladder and puts his hand on the edge of the hatch, and feels something soft, like cloth. Now something large and heavy is falling through the air towards him. He is being knocked off the ladder. The axe bounces and clanks as it slides from his grasp.

He looks up and covers his mouth to keep himself from crying out. Alan is hanged by the neck, arms limp, body broken. His fisherman's coat is draped around him like a shroud. His eyes are wide open and his mouth is wide open in a silent scream, and the rock is back from the tomb and the Redeemer is dead. He will not rise again.

I'll snap your bones you little bitch.

Violent severings. Trees whipping and bending.
Broken branches in the road, thick as a man's thigh.

chapter fourteen

i

The road in front of Laila's little Austin Metro: scattered with the woody victims of the storm. Violent severings. Trees whipping and bending. Broken branches in the road, thick as a man's thigh. Laila twists the wheel, swerving to avoid the debris, missing some but not all: dead wood crunches and thuds under the chassis. The hurricane has been building slowly all day. Laila and Ruth made hurried preparations to leave the house. Ruth stuffed her handbag with a thermos of coffee and jam sandwiches, and an athame: 'Never know when you might need it. Got me out of a dreadful scrape in '66.' Now, as they headed west towards Penzance, the tempest was bringing its full force to bear on the western lands. The motorway was blocked by a lorry blown onto its side so they were forced

133

to take smaller country roads. The hedgerows were rocking and bucking like lunatics at full moon but the little car made steady progress in spite of the storm's assault.

'We're coming up to Marshfield so we're not far from Somerset.' Ruth said. 'And so far, so good. No fallen tree blocking the road.'

Laila held up fingers tightly crossed.

'I have to admit, in all my years, I've never seen anything quite like this.'

'Are we in the eye of the storm?'

'This isn't a storm, my dear. It's a full-blown hurricane.'

Laila concentrated on the road. They were in the grip of a terrible enemy. Maybe her little Austin Metro wouldn't make it. Maybe it would be turned over like a Matchbox toy or crushed by a falling oak.

She wished she was back home in the warm, comfy flat she shared with Mindy. She thought of the familiar things she owned and loved - books, tea cups, her grandmother's quilt, her own bed. We sleepwalk through the best parts of life, she thought. She hadn't phoned anyone before setting off; now Mindy, her mum and dad, would be worried about her. She glanced sideways at the old trooper beside her - lionheart or lunatic, she couldn't decide. At the very least, she was a brave lunatic, and Laila drew courage from that.

Large spots of rain started to fall, dull and heavy against the windscreen. Laila flipped on the wipers. The rain smeared like syrup. It was harder and harder to see the road. The rain was congealing. She slammed on the brakes and the car slewed across the tarmac and pitched up onto the grass verge.

'Are you all right?' Laila asked, turning to Ruth.

'Oh, yes, I'm fine.' Ruth stared at the windscreen covered in the dark liquid: 'Apart from the blood.'

'Blood?' Laila said. 'How is that possible?'

'Powerful forces. They mean to stop us at all costs. They want to feast on those men on Devil's Rock. Sate themselves on terror and despair.'

'But why blood?'

Ruth's eyes widened: 'The Plagues of Egypt. They're playing with us, mirroring God's actions when the Pharaoh prevented the Israelites from fleeing Egypt. Oh good grief,' she said. 'There were ten plagues of Egypt.'

'What were they?'

'Locusts, flies, pestilence. I don't remember them all.'

Laila fixed her gaze back on the road. She turned the wipers to high and the windscreen cleared. She threw the car into gear and put her foot down. The blood rain was over.

ii

'I'm not sure how effective it will be,' Jabe said, taking two oil lamps from Brenda and placing them inside the optic. 'But it's something.' There had been no sign of Norton - or Spooky come to that. Brenda had been the only one willing to help him get Alan's body down from the lantern. Now it was covered with a blanket, lying in state by the station batteries. The engine room was cold as a mortuary. Jabe noticed the smell, like raw meat - was that what death smelled like?

'You look like shit,' Brenda said.

'Thanks,' he said. 'We should get back to the others.'

'Let's take a minute.' Brenda said. 'I'm not a big fan of

Cooper Reid or his jibes, or his arguments with Vanessa.'

'I don't want to stay in here though… with…' Jabe couldn't look at Alan's body again.

iii

They sat on the floor of the sleeping quarters instead, resting their backs against the wall.

'You said there was something not right about this Norton guy? Is that why he killed the skipper?'

'Alan.' Jabe said carefully. 'His name is Alan.' He fought to keep the emotion out of his voice. 'The skipper's name *was* Alan. It was Spooky… Cyrus, the acting PK, who thought there was something supernatural about Norton. How could anyone survive so long in the sea? And there was something about the way he moved. I think he was right. Alan didn't. Alan was very… rational.

'Norton said things that my dead father used to say. Word for word. There was no coincidence. My father was a completely amoral, evil man.'

Brenda said nothing for a moment. 'This is all pretty far out.'

'It's the truth.'

'It's fricking wild, but…' She looked at Jabe, searching his face for something, finding it. 'Your skipper - Alan - had you worked with him long?'

'Not very long.'

'Did he have family?'

'A wife and two kids.'

'Christ.' Brenda pictured the moment the news would be broken. 'That's awful. The kids must be quite young.'

'Teenagers.' Jabe took a deep breath.

136

How tenderly Jabe had held Alan's head in his hands. As Brenda watched him cover Alan's broken body, his grief had been an apparent immensity, a terrible and complete thing. A tear rolled down Jabe's cheek and he dashed it away hurriedly. Brenda saw the Pieta in her mind's eye, and understood now.

'You were close to him weren't you?'

He nodded and looked down. 'At least... I felt close to him. I don't know if he...'

'It's okay,' she said. 'Believe me, I know how it can be.' They sat there for a while, hearing the sounds of Cooper and Vanessa's bickering voices drifting up from below. 'You're sure there's no way we can contact the mainland?' Brenda asked.

'Absolutely.'

'We can't just wait around for Norton to pick us off one by one.'

'We can't get off the rock, your yacht's smashed up. What do you suggest?'

'It ain't my yacht, sugar. I am way more than that.'

iv

'You're a good-looking piece, love, but you're also one stupid bloody bitch.' Cooper never bothered to hide his irritation. 'You don't actually believe that some walking dead guy killed the skipper?'

'I don't know what to believe,' Brenda replied icily. 'But there's obviously something strange going on.'

'There's nothing 'strange' going on, love.' Cooper said, planting his hands on his hips. 'I know exactly who killed the skipper.' He pointed at Jabe. 'He did!'

'How d'you work that out?' Jabe said indignantly. He thought Cooper must be paranoid from too much booze and drugs.

'Listen sunshine. I don't know how or why you did it but you're the only one left alive in this hellhole. Ergo, you killed your boss, and possibly the other guy. Only you didn't have time to get rid of the second body before we turned up.'

'That's crazy.' Brenda said. 'He couldn't have killed the skipper. The guy's much bigger than him.'

'Maybe he coshed him on the back of the head.'

'His neck was broken. No one hit him on the back of his head.'

'I don't know how he did it, but I'm bloody sure he did.' He pivoted towards Vanessa. 'What do you think?'

'What do you want me to say, Cooper?'

'How about, Cooper you're right.'

'Cooper, you're right.'

Brenda nudged Jabe. 'Is there anything we can use to barricade the entrance to the tower?'

'No need to barricade - the doors have iron braces to keep the sea out.'

'Let's search the place, then. If we find Norton, we take him down. If not, it means he's outside, so we lock the doors and keep him out.'

'Hey, hey, hey!' Cooper said. 'Who put you in charge?'

'We need to do something.' Brenda said. 'Do you have a better idea?'

Cooper looked at her resentfully. 'Okay, here's what we'll do. Me, you and the boy will search the tower for this Norton guy. If he exists. Vanessa will stay here.'

'Fine by me, captain.' Vanessa said, waving the wine

bottle in salute.

'Maybe you should lay off a bit, darling?' Cooper took the bottle from her. He motioned to Brenda and Jabe. 'You two lead the way.'

As soon as Jabe's head is turned, Cooper raises the bottle and hits his mark - glass on skull - and it's like Jabe folds up before he collapses onto the floor.

'Now that's how you cosh someone,' Cooper says.

'What the hell did you do that for?' Brenda leans over Jabe. 'He's out cold.'

Cooper pulls a flare gun from his belt. 'Found this little lifesaver while you two were upstairs. Now we're going to do things my way.'

He was every inch the rock star.

chapter fifteen

i

Vanessa fastened Jabe's hands behind his back. She laced the rope around the spindles in the back of the chair then tied his feet together.

'You're wrong, Reid,' Brenda said grimly. 'This boy didn't have anything to do with the death of the skipper.'

'We'll see.' Cooper waved the flare gun towards Vanessa. 'You stay here and keep an eye on sleeping beauty. We'll check a floor at a time but I'd lay odds our killer's sitting right there.'

Brenda took Jabe's torch gently out of his pocket and picked up two oil lamps from the table. 'We'll need some light on the lower floors.'

'I was going to say that.' Cooper grabbed a couple of lamps as well. He looked over at Vanessa. 'Try to stay focused, darling,' he said. 'And shout if you need anything.'

'I've got everything I need.'

Cooper gave her a tight smile.

Then he was dislodging a little of the dark with the beam of his torch. Now he was pushing open the door of the lower engine room and casting light over the long-silenced workings of the Lister engines.

The light plays weakly on ducts, conduits, pipes. It's difficult to tell if it's just the light moving. Or imagination or something else. Then something definitely moves: the devil in the darkness, swift, deadly. Brenda shouts and stumbles. Cooper catches her as oil canisters clatter to the floor, dislodged and turning over, and the moment is broken.

'Just some rusty old oil drums,' Cooper says. 'Jesus!

Brenda lit one of the lamps and placed it carefully on the floor. The oil flame fluttered gently, casting jaundiced light over engine housings, rising pipework, manifolds. They lit another lamp on their way to the winch room.

At the base of the tower: no sign of Norton or the missing Cyrus 'Spooky' Jones. Brenda took boat rope from a hook and hung up the final lamp.

'Like I said,' Cooper told her smugly, hooking the flare gun back in his belt. 'There's no one lurking in the shadows. Never was. The kid is our killer.'

'I don't think so. And you shouldn't have hit him. We may need him.'

'Self-defence, my love. I got him before he got us.'

Brenda ignored Cooper and she sized up the exit.

'What are you doing?' Cooper asked.

'Going outside to check.'

'You've swallowed that bullshit story about some walking dead guy?'

'I don't buy the idea that Jabe's the murderer so we're even.'

'It's bullshit. Trust me.' He flashed a grin. This assessment of the situation seemed to relax him. 'And call me Cooper.' He moved closer, eased his arm round Brenda's waist and she slipped out of his grasp and through the doors. 'Okay,' he said. 'I can take a hint.'

The sea was tearing itself up over the rocks. The wind ripped the clouds to shreds, revealing a watery moon. Brenda peered into the distance, scanning the rocks for signs of movement. Something glinted in the agitated moonlight and its soft glinting caught her eye. She turned it over in her hands: a fingernail with part of the nail bed still attached to the underside.

'Whatcha got there?' Cooper came up beside her and she dropped it into his palm. 'Jesus Christ!' he said, flinging it away. 'The missing keeper. Maybe the kid killed him out here.' Brenda ignored him. 'Look at the state of my bloody yacht,' he said.

'Look on the bright side. You survived.'

'There's some very precious cargo on that wreck. Retrieve it, and I'll make it worth your while.'

'Why me?'

'You're staff, love.'

'I cook and clean, and help sail your goddam boat. That's all.' She looked up at the tower. 'We should get back inside.'

'All right, my Nubian princess.' Cooper wasn't sure if

Brenda had heard him; she was already walking away. He caught her shoulder. 'Wait,' he said and pulled out a ready-rolled spliff from his pocket. He cupped his hands round it and, on the second attempt, lit it. He inhaled deeply and passed it to her.

'There you go. Might make you less prickly.'

Brenda took it.

'It's good weed,' she said.

'Only the best.'

'You know, maybe you're right,' Brenda said. 'There sure doesn't seem to be anyone else on this rock,'

'I am right. The kid may be scrawny but wackos have incredible strength. I reckon he took the skipper unawares.'

'But why would he do it?'

'Maybe he just lost it. This place is enough to make anyone lose it. The kid couldn't take it anymore, finally snapped. Went loony.'

'Maybe so.'

'Only a nutjob would come up with the crazy story he's been telling.'

Brenda studied Cooper as he took another long drag on the spliff then handed it back to her again. She never imagined she'd be stranded on a rock in the Atlantic sharing a joint with someone like him.

She'd been working as a commis chef at a Turkish restaurant in Soho. Health inspectors closed the place down when a customer saw a rat by the kitchen. With no job and only the four walls of her Tottenham bedsit for company, she jumped at the chance to sail away to the Med. Not long into the voyage, she discovered how impossible Cooper could be. He was every inch the rock

144

star. Calling her out of bed in the early hours to make him a lobster sandwich or chips and curry sauce. Sending food back because the prawns were overcooked or the steak was underdone or the Hollandaise sauce 'tasted funny'. She almost threw in the towel when the boat moored at La Rochelle, only she didn't have the cash for the air fare home and her bank account was way overdrawn. At least she met Buster. He taught her a lot about sailing: maintaining proper sail trim; using the sheet and winch to control the amount of slack in the jib; staying low, keeping hold of the tiller and ducking under the swinging boom. Brenda liked and admired Buster. He was a good captain. Then Buster's skull had an argument with a bulkhead when the yacht struck the rocks. Now he was dead, his body covered by a blanket, just like the skipper of Devil's Rock lighthouse.

ii

The living quarters swam gradually into focus. Splashes of light danced at the periphery of Jabe's vision. Vanessa was sitting opposite him, picking at the label on a wine bottle.

'What happened?' Jabe croaked.

'Welcome back, honey. I thought you were a goner for a minute there.'

Jabe tried to touch his aching head but his hands were tied behind his back.

'Hey, what's going on?'

'My boyfriend slugged you. Hard. He thinks you're a murderer.'

'He's crazy.' Jabe tried to stand but his feet were also

tied. 'Come on, let me go.'

'Can't do that, I'm afraid.' Vanessa looked at him with a blend of excitement and unease. 'There's no telling what you might do.'

'Where's Brenda?'

'She's gone with Cooper to see if there really is anyone else on this rock.'

'There is and it's not human; it's something else and they're in terrible danger.'

'So says you.' Vanessa pointed a finger at him. For a brief moment her booze-addled brain remembered the details of his story and she almost began to believe it.

'I'm telling the truth,' he said. He had to keep her occupied while he worked on getting free. She stood up and went to the cupboard.

'Bingo!' She produced a wine glass. 'Any more drink around here?'

'Under the sink.'

'Yay!' Vanessa pulled out a bottle of Lambrusco, eyeing it scornfully. 'Christ. You and your mates aren't exactly connoisseurs but needs must...' She filled the glass then sat down again. 'So why's a nice boy like you working in a godforsaken place like this?'

'I like the isolation.'

'Girlfriend dump you?'

'Not exactly.'

'What you need is a real woman. Someone with experience.' Vanessa's eyes were bleary and she was taking great care not to slur her words. 'I haven't been with a younger guy for a long time. Cooper's so clapped out he can barely keep it up even when he manages to get it up.' She eyed him knowingly. 'Maybe we could have some fun together - before we all buy it on this rock.'

'How long have you and Cooper been together?' Jabe changed the subject.

'D'you know, I can't exactly remember. Hey, how far's Penzance from here? We were sailing to Penzance... I think... Penzance. Cooper's got a mate there who's going to look after some stuff we brought back from the Continent.' Vanessa raised an unsteady finger to her lips. 'Very hush, hush.'

'Drugs?'

'Just for personal use, you know. And there's some other stuff. Lots of cash. Cash Cooper doesn't want Nigel Lawson getting his hands on.'

'You weren't that far from Penzance when you ran onto the rocks.'

Vanessa didn't seem to hear him. She went to the pinup calendar and plucked it from the wall. She stood over Jabe and presented it to him. 'What's your favourite?' she asked.

'Eh?'

'What's your favourite month?'

'Oh, I dunno.'

'Go on.' She began flipping pages. 'Pick one. I'm interested to know. Call it market research.'

She turned at the sound of heavy, purposeful footsteps on the stairs. 'Cooper? Back so soon? Did you find your bogeyman?'

But it's not Cooper, of course. Bill Norton steps forward into the liverish light. Vanessa screams and drops the calendar. Norton's features are drawn up in a leery grin. His face is more decayed than before. Puss dribbles from points on his bluish-purple skin. He stinks like a collapsed

147

drain. Now he has her pinned against the wall.

'Oh Jesus! Get it the fuck off me!' She is swinging her arms furiously. He grips her head. He is pressing his thumbs into her eyes. Her scream rings down the tower. Now convulsions. Now blood streaming down her cheeks, her chin, her neck. Now Norton is turning her around. He snaps her neck with one swift jerk and her useless body drops to the floor. Her limbs jut awkwardly like a wrecked doll. Now Norton is turning to Jabe.

Cooper charges into the room. 'Jesus fucking Christ!' Cooper is kneeling beside Vanessa. 'Oh, God. No.' He looks up and here he starts whimpering. Norton towers over him. Now Norton is curling his fingers under Cooper's collar. Norton is hauling him to his feet. Cooper lashes out blindly. Cooper is landing punches on Norton's stomach and face.

'Hey, you ugly bastard.' Brenda calls to Norton from the doorway. Norton turns to look at her and Jabe recognises the expression. It is his father's leer. Norton is letting go of Cooper. Norton is drawn by Brenda out onto the landing. She delivers a kick. Norton tries to regain his balance. Brenda pushes him hard. Now he is falling. Now he is crashing down the stairs into the oily twilight.

Now there is no sound but the sound of the sea.

'Bloody hell.' Cooper said. 'Where d'you learn to kick ass like that?'

'I'm from Swansea.'

*She froze as Cooper aimed
the flare gun at the boy's head.*

chapter sixteen

i

Brenda hadn't known Vanessa that long - couldn't say
she cared for her that much but nobody deserved to die
like that. She felt an odd sort of regret that something
pretty had been damaged, wrecked. 'I checked the stairs,'
she said. 'He's gone.'

'He can't have just vanished.' Cooper said.

'Go see for yourself.'

Cooper returned her gaze warily. Brenda knelt behind
Jabe's chair and began untying him.

She froze as Cooper aimed the flare gun at the boy's
head. 'What the hell are you doing?'

'What the hell are *you* doing, love? I didn't say you could
untie him.'

'I don't need your permission. The real killer is out there

right now - we need all the help we can get.'

'How do you know they aren't working together?'

'Oh come on, Cooper. You saw the guy! He's a walking cadaver.'

'All I know is my woman is dead and junior's buddy killed her.'

'It was going to kill me next.' Jabe said.

Brenda stepped in front of Jabe, squaring herself up to Cooper and folding her arms. 'This is ridiculous. If you're going to shoot him, you'll have to shoot me first. Right now you look a lot more dangerous than he does.'

Cooper hesitated a moment then, with a quick, defiant gesture, he lowered the pistol. Brenda untied Jabe's feet and then his hands.

'Thanks.' Jabe rubbed his wrists.

She shut the door and wedged a chair tightly against the door handle. 'In case our friend decides to pay us another visit.' Jabe covered Vanessa's face with one of the waterproof jackets.

'Hey, what's this?' Cooper held up the ouija board.

'That's what started the whole mess.' Jabe said. 'We were messing around with it when the power went out.'

'If that was the start of it,' Brenda said, 'maybe it can help us put a stop to it.'

'This is bullshit.' Cooper said.

'What do you suggest instead?' Brenda asked him.

Cooper chewed his lip, glared at her broodily then walked to the window. 'I don't fucking know. Jesus, why does this shit always happen to me?'

Brenda ignored him and nodded to Jabe. He found the planchette and placed it in the centre of the board. Cooper protested but joined them nevertheless and lit another spliff.

'Empty your mind.' Jabe said, just as Spooky had begun. 'We are calling the spirits. Any spirit that is here.'

Nothing.

'Carry on.' Brenda said.

'We call on the spirits. Is anybody there?'

Nothing.

Cooper snorted.

'Is anybody there?'

The planchette began to move across the board. As before, the temperature in the room fell precipitously. Frost laced the brickwork. As before, the spirit would not give its name. 'What do you want?' Jabe asked.

S-T-O-P-H-I-M.

'Stop who?'

R-U-F-U-S.

'How do you know that name?' Jabe's voice faltered as he spoke.

S-T-O-P-H-I-M-S-T-O-P....

'Are you still there? How do you know that name?'

S-T-O-P-H-I-M...S-T-O-P...Y-O-U-R-F-A-T-H-E-R

Now he was running away, running down a familiar hallway. Now he had made it to the stairs but his feet were sinking through each step because the staircase was made of gum. He looked back and saw his father advancing, his face outlandish with loathing. Jabe grabbed hold of the banister but it was coated with oil. His fingers slid impotently against the slick and slippery wood.

'Little Twiggy! Little bitch! I'll snap your bones, you worthless piece of shit.'

The knife lay on the floor between them. Jabe tried to take

153

hold of the handle but it slipped out of his grasp and his father caught it. Rufus Walker eased an arm around his son's waist, pulling him close to him like a lover, holding the long knife to his throat...

Brenda guided Jabe back to the ouija board and the planchette. Jabe was no longer anchored securely in his own body. Something had broken free and what was left was an actor going through the motions in a long-running play. He was watching himself from without, watching Brenda and Cooper.

'How do we stop Rufus?' asked Brenda.

No response.

Then, gradually, the planchette began to move again.

C-A-S-T-H-I-M-B-A-C-K.

'Back where?'

F-R-O-M-W-H-E-R-E-H-E-C-A-M-E.

'Into the sea?'

YES.

'Is that the only way?'

H-E-A-D.

'What does that mean?'

Jabe was trembling, and the planchette trembled in sympathy. 'Mum?' he whispered. 'Is that you?'

Nothing.

He broke the link.

Cooper began a slow round of applause. 'Great performance. BAFTA-worthy!'

'Knock it off, Cooper.' Brenda told him.

'No, I mean it.' Cooper raised his eyebrows. 'He should audition for RADA. And you need your head felt if you believe one word of that crap. I know exactly what's going on. The supposedly 'missing' keeper - Spooky Jones - killed

Vanessa and the skipper. He's in cahoots with junior here. The ouija board stunt is to throw us off the scent. Are we seriously supposed to believe his dear old dad has possessed a drowned guy and brought him back to life? And now mommie dearest is sending messages from beyond the grave? I say we tie him up again.'

'I say we concentrate our efforts on finding a way to chuck Norton back into the sea,' said Brenda.

'If we could get him up to the lantern,' Jabe said, 'we could throw him off the south side straight into the sea.'

'How the fuck is that going to work?' Cooper exploded. 'And forgive me if I don't have a great deal of confidence in your leadership skills, love, but you said we should search the tower and next thing my woman is dead.'

'We have to try something. Or we're just sitting ducks.'

'Count me out.'

'I kind of figured that.'

'And by the way darling, you're sacked.'

Jabe turned to Cooper abruptly. 'Did you have electrical failure before you struck the rocks?'

'What? No! We were being tossed about like a cork but everything was working.

'The radio on the Snowgoose! How can we have been so slow?'

'There's one problem,' said Brenda. 'Norton.'

ii

'I'll go.' Cooper said. Brenda and Jabe couldn't conceal their surprise. Cooper pulled out the flare gun. 'I've got protection. I'll go and grab some of my valuables from the yacht and radio for help. And while I'm gone, you two can

155

capture your zombie and chuck him off the top.'

Jabe and Brenda traded glances. 'You've changed your tune. Why so helpful so suddenly?' she said.

'I still don't trust junior here, for one thing. And if this Norton geezer fucks up the pair of you, I'll stick by the radio and wait until the coastguard turns up.' He waved the gun. 'And like I said, I've got protection.'

'Nice to know you've got our best interests at heart.'

'If you want to reconsider, darling, tie him up and you and me can make sweet music together.'

'I'm tone deaf.' Brenda said.'

The petrol station was an island of light
in the whipping and reeling dark.

chapter seventeen

i

The petrol station was an island of light in the whipping and reeling dark. A solitary car crawled slowly through the night. Laila killed the engine.

'I need to make a call,' she told Ruth. 'My folks will be worried sick.'

'Of course,' Ruth said warmly.

'Do you need to call anyone?' Laila asked as she fumbled in her purse for coins.

'Oh no, I'm fine, my love. You run along.'

The whole phone box trembled violently in the wind. She dialled her parents' house. The line was engaged. She tried the flat. After several seconds, Mindy picked up.

'Oh, thank God you're all right. Where on earth are you?'

159

'I'm making my way down to Penzance.'

'What on earth are you doing down there?'

'It's a long story. Can you try and get through to my mum and dad, and just let them know I'm okay?'

'Sure. They've already been on the phone.'

'Just tell them I'm all right.'

'What's going on? You're not running away for a dirty weekend?'

'Of course not.' Laila laughed. 'Just tell everyone that I'm okay and I'll be in touch again soon.'

'But...'

The pips sounded and they were cut off. Laila hurried back to the car.

'Everything all right, dear?'

'Yeah. Everything's fine. Let's fill up.'

Newspapers flip-flopped across the tarmac. The forecourt canopy creaked ominously overhead. Laila thrust the nozzle into the tank. Ruth got out of the car, clinging to the doorframe to steady herself in the wind.

'Stay inside.' Laila called above the howling.

'No, no, no, dear. I'll go and pay.'

Without waiting for a response, Ruth pulled her coat tightly around her and made unsteadily for the shop. Pots of geraniums had fallen over and their red petals put her in mind of blood amongst the shards of broken terracotta. The door jangled cheerfully as she closed it behind her against the wind. The chiller cabinets buzzed and flickered erratically. A half-eaten tuna sandwich curled on a paper plate beside the cash register. Ruth guessed the attendant must be out back. Crisp packets and toilet paper were strewn in the aisle. It looked like the aftermath of a kinky party. She rang the bell on the countertop.

The fluorescent lights ticked - tick - tick - tick - the light was underpowered, intermittent and greenish. Ruth saw Laila replacing the petrol nozzle in its holder. Laila nodded as she got back into the car and Ruth waved in acknowledgement. She rang the bell again.

'Hello! Is anyone around?'

The florescents ticked on - tick, tick tick.

'I need to pay for some petrol.'

Tick - tick - tick.

Ruth started to feel unwell. Images appeared in her mind's eye: cannibalism in Bergen-Belsen; the Zeebrugge ferry disaster; Ian Brady, Dennis Nilsen, youth, innocence raped and murdered, the rotting stink of depravity and death. Like a rubbernecker at a motorway pileup, she felt compelled to see what was out back.

'Hello?' She walked to the back of the shop

Tick - tick - tick.

'Is anyone here?'

Tick - tick - tick.

She reached out for the door handle.

Tick - tick - tick.

She opened the door to a mean little staffroom with threadbare sofa, portable TV, broken coffee table, a little shattered glass on the floor.

Tick - tick - tick.

She opened the door to what looked like a meat locker.

Tick - tick - tick.

The air inside was sickly-sweet. She heard laboured breathing. Something whimpered.

'Hello?'

Tick - tick - tick.

She walked in the direction of the whimpering.

Tick - tick - tick.

She felt afraid. Pull yourself together, old girl, she thought. She straightened her spine, making herself as tall as she could.

Tick - tick - tick.

'Who's there? Are you all right?'

Tick - tick - tick.

A man's back. A man hunched over on the floor.

Tick - tick - tick.

'Can I help you, dear?'

Tick - tick - tick.

The man rises on his haunches. In the half-light, Ruth sees he is slick with sweat. The skin of his neck is very swollen. There are black masses - Ruth knows these are buboes. From her history books Ruth knows without any doubt that this is Bubonic Plague.

'Help me!' The man heaves the words from his swollen-to-split throat. Then he starts towards her.

Ruth backs down the aisle carefully but she still manages to catch her ankle. She snatches at shelves, boxes, cans - anything to stop herself from falling onto the concrete floor. The diseased man's breathing is quick, staccato. Greenish saliva wets his chin. He is reaching out to her with bloated and blackened fingers.

As if from nowhere, Laila is behind her, preventing her fall, dragging her by the arm to the fire exit. She lunges at the fire door but the bar does not depress, and the door doesn't open and all the while the lights are ticking tick - tick - tick.

The infected man is close now.

Tick - tick - tick.

162

He is going to speak.

Tick - tick - tick.

'They're all going to die. You'll never save them. Little bitch.'

Laila pumps the bar of the fire door.

Tick - tick - tick.

Kicks at the door wildly.

Tick - tick - tick.

Screams at it to open.

Tick - tick - tick.

Tick - tick - tick.

Tick - tick - tick.

And out they stumble onto the forecourt.

Now the sky is full of a different sound. The wind joined by something else.

'Flies!' Ruth mouths. 'Flies now!'

Now heavenly hosts of bluebottles are stroking, touching, feeling, tasting the car. Now they are pushing their way in through the air vents. Laila thrusts the key into the ignition. The car lurches and stalls. The song of the bluebottle fills the car. Ruth tries to cover the grills with her hands but the heavenly host are too many. Laila turns the key again. The engine kicks into life and she starts the windscreen wipers and the bluebottles rise to avoid the blades and settle again, and rise and settle. Laila drives blindly out onto the road. She tries the screen wash and looks in the rearview mirror and sees the filthy cloud filling the forecourt but not moving out onto the road.

'More plagues of Egypt?' she asks.

'Pestilence and swarms of flies.' Ruth says. 'With more to come.'

ii

The sea breathed into the tower and out again. Cooper had left the doors wide open and Jabe was looking out at the blind chaos of the sea. 'How are we going to get Norton into the tower and up to the lantern?' he asked.

'Lure him with noise.'

Brenda squared herself, then swung the fire axe hard. It connected with the gunmetal, creating a resounding crack like a pistol shot.

This was the moment and she felt it urgently. She swung the axe again and once more the sound, sharp as glass, reverberated through the night. If anyone was out there, they couldn't fail to hear her.

'Norton!' she yelled. 'Rufus Walker! Come on you bastard. We're waiting for you!'

*He knew exactly who she was – he'd ogled
her picture often enough on Page Three.*

chapter eighteen

i

Ahead lay the wrecked Snowgoose. Cooper smiled to himself: it would be good to get out of the wind at least. He just had to rest a little longer, huddled in the wind-shadow of the rock. Vanessa was dead. Life gone and done with before time. Here. Now not here. They had met at the Limelight - the release of *Davey and the Shakers' Greatest Hits* - courtesy of his record label. Her obvious youth drew Cooper, and her perfectly rounded, perfectly large breasts. He knew exactly who she was - he'd ogled her picture often enough on Page Three.

She put on a world-class performance for the paparazzi: pouted and pushed her hair up, and arched her back to thrust out her most valuable assets. But away from the photographers, she was surprisingly coltish, and Cooper had the impression in some ways she was a hostage to her own fame. Her awkward vulnerability ramped up the attraction. He knew he had to have her.

A one night stand was what he had in mind. He certainly wasn't looking for anything more - he already had two failed marriages under his belt. He was the band's lead guitarist and one of the star attractions at any party: it didn't take long before she noticed him. And it didn't take long for him to win her over. He took her to The Ivy for a slap up dinner then on to his flat in Bywater Street, just off the King's Road. Climbing into the taxi, she turned her head and smiled and the thought of her hard young body underneath the red cocktail dress aroused him so that he pulled her close clumsily, and kissed her cherry lips. He imagined all the things he wanted to do to her. He was so drunk everything passed by in slow motion. He remembered lying on top of her but that was all. He must have passed out.

The next morning she woke him up with breakfast in bed. Badly cut toast and watery Nescafé. He ran his fingers gently over the silk-skin of her thighs. His hangover competed with the swelling between his legs, and the hangover lost. He pushed her thighs apart and rolled in between them, cupping and kissing her generous breasts. They made love again and again that day, and slept, and watched videos, and ordered takeaway. Behind the come-to-bed eyes, he could see she was ambitious. She craved the spotlight as much as he did but she wasn't yet accomplished enough to handle all that went with it. He could teach her. He knew he had to see her again.

They soon developed an unspoken contract: she wanted a rock-star boyfriend and he wanted a glamour model on his arm. Over the months, their rocky relationship kept them on the front pages of the tabloids. As the sex failed, it was their need to be noticed and recognised that held them together. Fame was everything. And now she was dead, and all that was done, and he was stuck on this godforsaken rock, huddled out of the wind. At least if he died here, it would make for one helluva rock 'n' roll legacy to rival Buddy Holly or Johnny Kidd. But Cooper Reid wasn't ready to join the legions of the rock 'n' roll dead just yet. He loved his drugs, his women and his back catalogue too much.

ii

He moved slowly and deliberately up over the rugged rise into the wind and on towards the Snowgoose. He climbed the stern ladder and edged carefully across the helm, stopping dead when the floorboards protested squeakily underfoot. He pulled out the flare gun, just in case. The boat rocked in the wind and he had to steady himself as he climbed down into the saloon. He flicked on the lights. The whole interior was tilted forty-five degrees as the boat knocked and groaned against the rock. Seawater ran across the floor now this way, now back, now this way again.

Cooper found Buster's dead body where he and Brenda had left it. He had actually liked his elderly captain. Now he was simply a corpse on the bed Cooper and Vanessa had shared. Poor beautiful, dead Vanessa. He eased himself down the steps into the galley. An empty wine bottle rolled across the floor in the master cabin and clunked in rhythm with the rocking boat.

Water and debris filled the far end of the cabin. The yacht was no match for the sea's casual brutality and the little room had been violated absolutely by the rising tide. Cooper retrieved a small attaché and flicked it open. The case was crammed with money: two hundred and fifty thousand British pounds. And two bags of cocaine. 'Hello my lovelies,' Cooper whispered, running his fingers over the wads of notes. 'Papa's come back for you.' He closed the case and made his way back through the galley. He crossed the saloon to the port side and checked the radio. It was working. But first things first: he had to pee. He hooked the flare gun back in his belt, unzipped his fly, put one hand on the wall to steady himself and aimed into the corner. The warm spattering jet eased the pressure on his bladder and he sighed. He shook himself off, zipped back up, touched his belt lightly to make sure the flare gun was still at his side. He liked the feel of a weapon. Any kind of weapon. Then he turned to go.

A man was levelling a harpoon at his chest.

'Jesus fucking Christ!' Cooper said.

'Stay right there pal.'

'Who the fuck are you? What the fuck are you doing on my boat?'

'I'll ask the questions.'

The man was thin with a goatee moustache and hair pulled back in a ponytail. He looked mad with fear and dangerous in equal parts. He must have been hiding in the portside cabin.

'Are you Jones?' Cooper asked. 'The other keeper.'

'Shut up.'

'Calm down. I only came back here to use the radio.'

Spooky Jones, Principal Keeper, took a couple of steps

170

back and nodded towards the attaché case. 'What's this?'

'Things I needed to pick up.'

'Open it.'

'Look, mate, we're on the same side. I don't have any beef with you. I'm just trying to get away from that crazy motherfucker in the tower.'

'Open the case.' Spooky said. 'Now.' His grizzled head was snapping from Cooper to the case and back again. Cooper could see he had to play it cool. He held up his hands in a conciliatory gesture.

He makes a great show of opening the case, but throws it across the cabin instead. The force jabs Spooky sharply in the abdomen. He drops the harpoon, grunting and curling over, and Cooper charges at him, sending them both sprawling down the aisle, an angry mess of arms and legs. Now Cooper is on his back underneath Spooky and he puts his arms up to protect his head from the keeper's blows. A shadow slides into the cabin and stops in the doorway above them. Norton grabs Spooky by his pony tail, lifting him smoothly into the air. Spooky scrabbles and whines. Norton takes Spooky's head between his powerful hands and snaps his neck. Spooky pitches forwards. His body lands on top of Cooper and it's a dead weight, shunting the air out of Cooper's lungs. Now Norton's head is dancing on the stump of his neck like a mamba about to strike. Cooper is pinned down, urgent fingers casting about for the flare gun. Norton reaches down in one fluid movement and is about to press his thumbs into Cooper's eyelids.

'No wait! Please! I can help you. I know it's not me you want. It's the boy.'

171

The smoke is changing, now black, now tarry.
It is an expanding mass of asphyxiation and death.

chapter nineteen

i

Norton hisses. 'Speak!' The voice is a death rattle.

'They're going to throw you off the tower. Into the sea. They know its the only way to end this. To send you back.' With one powerful stroke, Norton lifts Spooky's corpse free of Cooper and tosses it aside.

'You want to live?' Norton's lopsided grimace reveals fallen teeth and livid gums.

'I've told you what I know. Please, just let me go.'

'I can't.'

'Have mercy.'

'*M-e-r-c-y?*'

Norton pulls him to his feet. They are face to face. Cooper smells Norton's dead breath. Norton sees through him to the inconsequential little flame of his soul.

173

Cooper's searching fingers find the flare gun and he thrusts it into Norton's chest, but Norton's preternaturally strong hand closes around his own. Slowly Norton turns the gun. Norton's fingers slide around the trigger. Norton is going to kill him. 'No!' Cooper whispers. Incredible heat enters his stomach, mounts up, roasts the contents of his chest cavity. Norton releases him and blood pours like gravy browning from his mouth. He looks up pleadingly. He is a petrified child and Norton is a fantastical horror, something that oughtn't to exist. Something that oughtn't ever to be seen, especially by a child. And now it is really happening: the monstrosity is digging Cooper's dying eyes out of his child's skull.

ii

Jabe swung one last time and the metal of the bulkhead screamed and yammered. He rested the axe on the ground and leaned back, wiping his forehead on his sleeve.

'That should be enough now,' Brenda said.

'You think he'll come?'

'He'll come.'

They waited in the lantern, just out of reach of the wind. Jabe hugged his knees close to his chest. 'He's going to kill us, all of us,' he said simply.

'We can't afford to think like that.'

'He'll wait us out.'

'No, he'll come now. He's a bloodthirsty bastard. He'll come up here and we'll throw him into the sea.'

'How will we do it?'

'Perhaps it won't come to that. Perhaps Cooper will

174

make it to the Snowgoose. If the radio's working, all our troubles might soon be over.' Brenda stared straight ahead. The boy's hopelessness was beginning to get to her.

Jabe took a deep breath. 'How did you get mixed up with Cooper in the first place?'

'He wanted a cook and I needed a job.'

'But Cooper.....'

Brenda smiled. 'A first class bastard most of the time. But I got to go to La Rochelle. And Buster taught me a lot about sailing. He was a good old guy. We'd sit out on deck on a clear night with tea and bacon sandwiches and watch the sea rolling in the moonlight. He'd tell me stories from his time in the navy.'

'What were Cooper and Vanessa doing?'

'What do you think? They weren't really seafaring types. A yacht was just a status symbol to Cooper: it went well with the trophy girlfriend. He had to pitch in but he was always on a short fuse. Vanessa was far too precious to get her hands or her Ralph Laurens dirty.'

'Who do you think spoke through the ouija?'

'You think it was your mother?'

'Yes.' Jabe tilted his head slightly as if straining to hear something - a whisper on the wind. 'Someone's looking out for us. I believe that.'

For a while neither of them said anything. Only the sea spoke; at first in the usual way - the rhythm of waves against rock and the great sucking back of the tide. But then it spoke to Jabe in another way, ringing and singing and getting merry: you-cannot-kill-what's-already-dead.

'Norton is saving me for last.' Jabe said. 'What if we screw up his plans for him - he can't kill me if I'm already dead!'

'You want me to kill you now?

'I want him to *think* you're going to kill me. Get up. I want to try something.' He pulled Brenda's arm round his chest. 'Imagine Norton up here in the lantern. He sees us like this, sees you about to kill me. What's he going to do?'

'He's going to come at us. Come at me.'

'Exactly. And at the last moment, we separate, and he's through us, moving fast, and almost over the rail - we just have to make sure he goes right over.'

They practised moving in sync with each other. It was like dancing with the Devil Brenda said, or fox-trotting not-to-get-fucked-over said Jabe, and they began to laugh. Jabe laughed in a way he hadn't since coming to Devil's Rock and Brenda caught it.

Beyond the walkway, under cover of night, the sea spat and hissed. High overhead, the stars were tracing their prescribed paths dutifully, saying, 'We give you the precession of the equinoxes - you're welcome!' Then something unusual happened: a star chuckled and moved out of turn. Over the far rim of the earth, the sun answered with its own kind of laughter. In the depths of the tower something was moving. Grey as a mouse, it was finding its way upwards from crevice to crevice, climbing steadily towards the gallery. It curled and stretched, searched and tested, felt its way into the engine room, a relentless, suffocating killer of men.

'Smoke!' shouted Jabe. 'Smoke! We have to get out now!'

Now an explosion shakes the tower! 'What the hell was that?'

'A and B engines have blown!' Jabe says. 'Norton has started a fire in the lower engine room!'

The smoke is changing, now black, now tarry. It is an expanding mass of asphyxiation and death. A solid shape, like the shape of a man and at the same time something different, rises through the centre. Norton is grinning. His teeth have all fallen. His hands are misshapen and bruise-black. Brenda backs away strategically. She is taunting him. Jabe breaks for the stairs. Brenda swings the axe but Norton evades the blow. The cold hard granite of the tower is at Brenda's back as Norton lunges. She twists cleverly and slams the axe into his side. He howls, heaving the axe from his rib cage and there is no bleeding. Norton is bloodless. Norton is a bloodless dead thing. Nothing is more important now than distance. The heat is worse. Flames leap and curl from the lower engine room. The room is awash with burning oil. Bags of cotton waste are blazing tinder. Jabe turns back to see Norton on all fours - a four-legged dead thing now - scuttling across the wall. A blast of heat and flame beats Norton back. This secondary explosion winds Brenda and Jabe, and Jabe croaks, 'What do we do now?', and tears are running down his smoke-stained face.

'We should go to the Snowgoose.'

The remaining babies were killed at predetermined intervals as the submarine travelled further and further from the shore.

chapter twenty

i

They hadn't expected to find Cooper dead. He had been too loud-mouthed, too self-obsessed, almost too obnoxious to die. They struggled to take in the scene on the Snowgoose: Cooper's eyes torn out of his skull. Nothing left to bear witness to the crime. Jabe and Brenda, the last ones standing against the insurmountable Norton.

Brenda checked the flare gun. It was empty.

Jabe found the attaché. 'Jesus. This is quite a haul.'

'Cooper Reid was a rich man.' Brenda retrieved the harpoon: a Greener Mark II - like a modified shotgun with a long metal dart instead of cartridges. 'This was Cooper's. Said he wanted to kill a shark with it one day. I managed to spear a few bluefin tuna in my time.'

Jabe concentrated on the radio. He checked the circuit

breaker then set the VHF to channel 16. He adjusted the squelch until the hissing subsided and then he keyed the mic, speaking slowly.

Mayday, Mayday, Mayday. Calling MRCC Falmouth, this is Devil's Rock. Over.

After a few seconds, the radio burst into life.

Devil's Rock, this is MRCC Falmouth. What is your emergency? Over.

We have multiple fatalities. We have total loss of power and a fire in the lower engine room. Request immediate rescue. Over.

Devil's Rock, please state number of casualties. Over

We have zero casualties. Multiple fatalities, including shipwrecked civilians. We are under attack from a hostile force. Over.

Please state the nature of the hostile force. Over.

Falmouth. We have a crazed and hostile individual on the loose. There are two of us left. We need immediate rescue. Over.

Roger, Devil's Rock. Helicopter on its way, ETA forty-five minutes. Over.

Brenda put her arms round Jabe. 'We're going home! Where will the helicopter land?'

Jabe pointed up to the flat circular structure at the top of the tower. 'That's the helicopter pad. We have to meet the chopper up there.'

'Right.' Brenda said, weighing the harpoon in her hands. 'Then we're definitely going to be needing this.'

ii

The windows of RN 771 Naval Air Squadron, Culdrose glowed in the early morning dark. A single bulb hung from the low ceiling of the mess hall. Next to the electric kettle, a Roberts RFM3 transistor radio was rattling out *Eyes of the Devil* by Dead Men Walking:

The Devil is smiling in the cold dark night,
Do you have the strength to fight this fight?

Haroon Bakshi leaned back in his chair and contemplated the cards in his hand. Then he looked at his two opponents. All three men were down from Portland on a training visit. The wind had been battering the helicopter base for several hours and nobody was able to sleep so they decided to wile away the time playing poker. Rescue services along the south coast were struggling to cope with the volume of calls coming in. Bakshi had a feeling his crew would be called on at any moment, even if it meant going up in the training helicopter.

It was difficult to judge what Rob Raiment was thinking, which was why he usually won at poker. Raiment's unreadable stare was currently fixed on Bakshi. Next to him was their new winchman, Alfie Judge. He was the youngest of the three, much less experienced at the games of poker and life. When his hand was weak he looked down. When he was nervous, the tips of his ears turned pinker. His hand *was* weak, but the real cause of his discomfort was the bad feeling in his gut, which made the skin on his balls crawl and shrivel.

Do you see the corpse with the cold dead stare?
No hope left now – only despair.

He'd been reading about Soviet scientists in the 1950s

experimenting on a female rabbit and her litter. The mother was confined to a laboratory with electrodes implanted in her brain. The litter were put on a submarine. As the submarine dived, the scientists killed the first of the litter. At the same moment, the mother's brain activity and heart rate peaked. The remaining babies were killed at predetermined intervals as the submarine travelled further and further from the shore. Each time, the mother's physiology responded violently. When the last of the litter was killed, she had a brain haemorrhage and died.

Judge had an inkling this could be his last night on earth. He told himself: stop being a pussy; but the feeling persisted.

Now you are falling, lost all hope,
Now you are hanging at the end of the rope.

Bakshi took another card from the pack and laid it next to the four already on the table. They placed their final bets, each sliding a pound note into the pile. Bakshi turned his cards face up: a pair of threes and a pair of fives. Judge had a pair of aces. Raiment paused, a smile playing on his lips as he looked at Bakshi and put his cards on the table: a pair of sevens and a pair of jacks. He reached across and lovingly scooped the pile of notes towards him.

The scramble bell rings. Seconds later the dispatcher appears and says, 'We're going to need you boys. Distress call from Devil's Rock. Immediate evac. Two people.'

The men are up already and at the lockers retrieving flying suits and emergency first aid. The dispatcher gives them the details. The three crewmen walk purposefully to the waiting chopper and begin their pre-flight checks.

'This is a first for me,' Bakshi says. 'A psychopath on a lighthouse.'

'It's got to be one of the civvies,' says Raiment.

'Someone like Michael Ryan.'

'Jesus, what an evil bastard.'

'Hey, Judge, you okay back there?' Bakshi checks - the younger man is all eyes as he nods and stares back at them. Judge has only been operational a couple of weeks and Bakshi isn't quite convinced he's up to the job yet. Bakshi raises an eyebrow at Raiment. Engine one is up and running. Bakshi starts up engine two. The fuel flow, engine oil and hydraulic pressure are all green. He sets the altimeter and requests clearance. The chopper judders as it lifts slowly into the dark fortress of a sky.

'Okay, boys,' Bakshi says. 'The storm's on the retreat but the winds are still strong. This is going to get a bit bumpy. Let's see what's out there.'

Judge looks like he's going to be sick. He joined the forces to please his father, a navy man himself - and very tough to please. Now, he's acutely aware of his own inexperience. He's done all his hours - but this is real life. He's the Junior Joe on the crew. He doesn't like real life and he's never seen a storm like this before. He rubs his palms together and swallows. He tells himself to concentrate on the job; get the job done but still something's eating away at him. Fear tastes like greasy metal at the back of his throat. He thinks about the baby rabbits on the Russian submarine, and the song on the radio:

The Devil is smiling in the cold dark night,
Do you have the strength to fight this fight?

The wind punches wildly at the chopper. Bakshi takes them low over the headland and out across the open sea. He grips the cyclic firmly, fighting to keep the aircraft steady. The retreating storm has a scorpion's tail. Gradually the lights of Culdrose fade and they are alone above the turning sea.

Now she is riding into the dark, pitching over the sea like a storm petrel forever in flight over the deep ocean.

chapter twenty-one

i

The little Metro's headlights picked out a road sign - Hayle, eight miles from Penzance. Laila was talking but Ruth wasn't replying. She was staring into the distance and she was deathly white.

'Are you alright?' asked Laila.

'Stop the car.' Ruth said. 'Stop the car! This place, this exact spot, will work to our advantage. We must stop here.'

'But we're almost at Penzance.'

'It's no good. We have to do something now. Things on Devil's Rock are coming to a head. Stop the car.'

Laila pulled off the road. 'This way,' Ruth said. She slipped through a gap in the hedgerow into a large field and the spectacular ruins of an old priory. Wind was pouring wildly through the canopy of the trees. The cold was a rain of cuts. Ruth held out her arms, turning methodically from side to side. She stayed like this for a long time as Laila looked on, uncertain whether to say anything or not.

Then Ruth was on the move again. She marched to the ruins, dropped to her knees in front of what would have been the priory's altar and placed her hands on the old stones. Laila crouched down next to her. No doubt ancient horrors had taken pace in the priory's ruins, little inquisitions and the ultimate defilement of The Reformation but Laila was glad of the little protection its broken stones gave them from the storm.

'What do we do now?'

'It's very simple, dear. We give them all the psychic help we can. This altar lies on a ley line. Ley lines connect places of remarkable power, the vital energies of the earth herself. We'll tap into that, surf on it, you might say, all the way out to Devil's Rock.'

'How did you know the ruins were here?'

'I didn't until a few moments ago. Now I need your help. You're very important because you have a direct emotional, and therefore psychical, connection to your friend. That will be invaluable in battling the forces that oppose us.'

'Whatever you say.' Laila told her. Ruth took hold of Laila's hand gently and instructed her to conjure a mental image of Jabe.

ii

Ruth felt herself rising upwards, riding a wave of psychic energy, as if ascending a staircase cut into the air.

188

She came level with the tree-canopy which was rocking and knocking like a wooden sea. She saw her own body below and Laila kneeling beside her.

Now in seven league boots she is striding over Buryas Bridge to St. Buryan, Sparnon, Porthcurno. The rocky peninsula offers up summits and reefs as it pushes out into the sea. Where Land's End stretches its limbs into the Atlantic, she passes over the notorious Runnel Stone, bringer of destruction to so many ships. Now she is riding into the dark, pitching over the sea like a storm petrel forever in flight over the deep ocean. On towards Devil's Rock.

Ruth feels her kinship with the forces of light and life. Beneath her the sea senses her presence and swells and shifts like a leviathan. She is unafraid. She is confident of her own rhythmic co-existence with creation itself.

In the far distance, she makes out - there! - a faint glow at the top of the tower. Here, she sees smoke spilling out of the lantern, now ripped away by the violence of the storm. Now she has arrived on Devil's Rock. She knows something is present, formless, coagulating, becoming. It has taken many shapes over thousands and thousands of years. Norton is an intelligent insect now, scuttling across the lighthouse ceilings, setting traps for his prey. He puts out the nearest oil lamp - a single gesture and the flame is choked to death - then scuttles off with intent to find the next lamp and do the same.

Ruth focuses her mind on the dead lamp. What is not quite dead can be brought back to life. What is dark can be awoken by the light. Slowly, steadily, the flame struggles back into existence: a little beacon, dancing unsteadily perhaps, but safe for the moment in its little glass chimney. Ruth finds the second extinguished lamp. Again, she gathers all her strength; the smoke circles steadily, increases in volume, pales, and the wick bursts back into life. It is difficult psychic work and she is unsure how long she can sustain it at such an extension from her physical body. Her vision blurs a little, begins to wobble and judder. Something is happening at the priory, affecting her physical body. If her physical body is threatened, her consciousness will be cast back suddenly and painfully from the astral realm.

Laila looks up. The ruins are meat and drink for the storm. The wind works hard at the dilapidated and venerable stones. Clouds stream across the sky, obscuring the brightness of the waiting moon. Lightning cuts the night. Hailstones start falling large as golf balls. Flints and mortar are falling from the high tower of the priory. Laila draws Ruth's earthly body out of harm's way to a niche in the breached walls, perhaps a nun's cell. She draws Ruth's earthly body gently to her and protects her with the warmth of her own body.

Ruth's concentration is wavering now. Her astral self is at full extension. It takes all her strength to warm another lamp and bring it back into the world of heat and flame. She intends to relight as many of the lamps as possible to light the way for what she perceives will be the final battle. But she is coming to the end. And the end is Norton, barring her way. He is a ruined creature, burned, broken and relentless. He is looking directly at her.

She wonders, briefly, if he can see her. And yes, he sees her. The Fall has come. It is clear what is good and what is evil. He moves so very quickly. She is falling from the

190

tower, from grace, from the astral world. A fit slams her back into her physical body. Pain blinds her momentarily. For a beat of time, she has no idea where she is. Is she at home? Is she in a cellar? And then she feels Laila's warmth and recognises her face. Laila is simply relieved Ruth is still alive.

'More plagues of Egypt,' Ruth whispered hoarsely. 'Thunderstorms of hail and fire.'

'Are you all right?' Laila asked.

'I've had better days. But I did all I could. It's up to Jabe now and whoever is with him.'

iii

Jabe and Brenda have only one aim now: to get to the helipad and get off Devil's Rock. An oil lamp burns faintly at the base of the tower and lights their way. Brenda grips the harpoon gun as if it's a reluctant lover. The light flickers over water tanks, crab pots, saltwater pumps. Norton has the advantage. He can choose his moment.

Vanessa's body hangs like a dead rabbit at a butchers: blonde hair matted and tangled, pale white breasts exposed and streaked with blood. She is the dead crow, strung up by the gamekeeper, as a warning. She is Norton's warning: this is what's in store for you; what vermin you are. At the sight of Vanessa, Jabe feels nothing at all - simply because he has become horribly accustomed to the spectacle of death.

Brenda nods grimly towards the engine room.

'We have to check. We don't want him coming up behind us.' Jabe's torch lights the doorway unsteadily.

191

Brenda counts silently to three then jerks the door open. The room is empty.

They carry on past the blood-coloured winch workings, the oil tanks and gauges. It's getting hotter. Patches of floor are still burning but at least the bitter smoke has cleared. Mostly. There is the rope Cooper used to tie Jabe up. There is dried blood. Vanessa's blood. Brenda eases open the door to the sleeping quarters. Alan's dead body has been stripped naked, eye sockets emptied of their contents. His genitals are missing - a special message for Jabe. Jabe has nothing left. He has run out of fight.

'He's trying to break us,' Brenda says. 'We can't let him.'

Jabe doesn't hear.

'We can't let him beat us,' she says gently.

He looks at her blankly, wiping at the tears falling silently down his cheeks. What good was any of it now? Norton was going to win. He had killed everybody else. Jabe had lost his faith in the idea of goodness, in the idea that decency would prevail. He was not afraid any more, just perniciously cynical. He was surprised how calm he felt. He had nothing to lose because everything was lost. And that changed things. After a few moments, he got slowly to his feet and nodded solemnly to Brenda.

iv

Brenda let the harpoon drop loosely at her side. 'Where the hell is he?' she whispered.

'Listen!' Jabe said. A loud thrumming sound outside, closer now. 'The rescue chopper.'

As the words leave Jabe's mouth, Norton appears from

192

nowhere. In one swift movement, he is on Brenda, and punctures her side between two ribs. He turns his fingers in the wound between the two bones and Brenda cries out in agony. Jabe has nothing to lose any more. He's watched his father almost kill his mother. Now the only reasonable person left in this hateful place is about to be killed. He lunges at Norton, which is not what Norton is expecting. 'Come on you bastard!' Jabe shouts, backing away, drawing him away from Brenda. 'Come on! It's me you want. Are you man enough? Come and get me... I'm the little bitch, remember... Little twiggy... little bitch is biting back!'

Norton is pure and fathomless fury as he comes for Jabe. The boy scrambles into the lantern, races out onto the gallery. He climbs the yellow ladder to the helideck, thrusts open the hatch, and hauls himself up onto the platform into the caterwauling wind. Except Norton has caught his ankle. He tries to kick free but Norton's dead-hand grip is strong as a mastiff's jaws. Jabe kicks him in the rotting head with his free foot - his got-nothing-to-lose bitch's foot - and Norton looks briefly bewildered as he falls back through the hatch like a dazed bluebottle in late summer...

The rescue chopper circles the platform and its down-draught is hammering the whole structure. Now Norton reappears at the hatch and he is holding the harpoon. He straightens up. He takes aim.

Captain Haroon Bakshi realises the danger too late. The harpoon smashes through the copter's windshield, opening Bakshi's chest. He slumps onto the cyclic. The chopper banks sharply to the left and hits the side of the tower. Masonry explodes. The chopper's blades shear off. The debris misses Jabe by some got-nothing-to-lose miracle and smashes through the safety netting that surrounds the platform.

The chopper turns and twists and rolls down the length of the tower. Jabe is scrambling across the helipad. Norton advances as the whole structure sways. Jabe is thrown violently across the platform over the side and lands in the safety netting. Below, the chopper's fuel tanks explode. A great plume of octane and burning debris rises up over the tower like a golden wave and burning fuel rains down, like God's retribution, onto the helideck. The helicopter's burning wreckage disintegrates on the rocks below. A massive roller sweeps over the rocks and leaves them clean as a picked bone.

Norton reaches down and worries the netting with his insect's claws. The netting resists for a while then gives way and Jabe is falling. He reaches out and somehow finds a handhold, and it is not the first miracle on Devil's Rock. A hundred and forty feet below, the furious sea waits as Norton works at prizing Jabe's fingers free. Now Norton is hissing and bobbing in triumph. Jabe looks into his eyes and they are his father's eyes.

Norton shouts, above the wind, 'I'll take you to hell with me, you fucking little bitch.'

And just like that, Norton's head leaves his body. Jabe sees Brenda, battered but not broken, fire axe in hand, and it is the great miracle of Devil's Rock. Norton's head is a deflating beach ball falling into the sea. Then his body pitches forward, as if in sympathy, and disappears into the black water.

The boundary between night and day was
softening once more as the autumn morning dawned.

epilogue

The boundary between night and day was softening once more as the autumn morning dawned. Daybreak gifted orange light to the cloudless sky. The storm had blown itself out and the legacy of its spent rage was destruction and havoc. Now it was being called a 'weather bomb' because of its sudden, rapid expansion and its devastating impact. The strongest winds had been recorded in the southeast - 120 miles an hour in Hampshire, Essex and Kent. Thousands of people were without power and children were waking up to the unexpected gift of a holiday from school. Parks, forests, roads and railway lines were closed, strewn with trees fallen like a bad game of Jenga. Nowhere was left unaffected by the violent abuses of the storm.

At Culdrose airbase, the wind had dropped to a whisper, its passion finally spent. Bare trees shivered in the morning light. A couple of miles from the coast, a helicopter was powering steadily towards the shore. Its distinctive red and white paint scheme asserted itself in the gathering light. Its rotor blades whipped overhead, hurrying it to the absolute certainty of solid land. A few minutes later, the chopper was turning, thundering across the shoreline. On the beach below, a man stopped to watch. At his heels, a black-and-white collie barked excitedly, then chased the shadow of the giant striped bird across the sand, giving up only as it disappeared over the headland. The helicopter descended deftly onto the naval base helipad. Two men climbed out, carrying a stretcher between them. They were accompanied by a much younger man, really no more than a boy. He walked alongside and held the hand of the injured woman.

'You're going to be okay,' Jabe told her, trying to sound reassuring. Brenda smiled shakily at him. As the two men loaded the stretcher into the waiting ambulance, Jabe looked across at the rolling countryside. Trees clothed the base of a low hill - grassy slopes and pretty cottages - meandering roads. It all seemed almost too beautiful. Soon the sun would climb higher in the sky and, if the day turned out to be as fair as it promised, the world would unfold against a canvas of ravishing blue.

'Jabe!'

He turned at the sound of the familiar voice and saw Laila running towards him. He'd never been so glad to see anyone. They hugged for a long while.

'What on earth are you doing here?' Jabe said.

'It's a very long story.'

'I'm glad you're here. Really glad.'

'Me too.'

The paramedics closed the ambulance doors.

'Where are you taking her?'

'Penzance Infirmary.'

'I'll drive you there,' Laila said. 'And there's someone I'd like you to meet.'

They made their way to Laila's battered Mini Metro. Ruth was sitting inside. She climbed out rather stiffly, leaning heavily on the door as Laila introduced her.

'I'm delighted to see you safe and sound and back on dry land.' Ruth said.

'So am I.' Jabe said.

'And I feel certain you've exorcised a particularly nasty demon.'

Jabe looked away, towards the departing ambulance.

'Your friend will be fine.' Ruth rested a hand on his shoulder. 'Ever since that monstrosity injured her in the tower, I've been with her all the way. Let's get off to the hospital where I hope we can each get a nice cup of tea.'

They got into the little Metro and Laila started the engine. The sun had climbed higher now as if heralding something; a waymarker to the future, to possibility, to life.

Page 106: Cottonbro Studio
https://www.pexels.com/photo/10640005

Page 112: Cottonbro Studio
https://www.pexels.com/photo/5028432

Page 120: David McElwee-
https://www.pexels.com/photo/13312223

Page 128: Vera Silkina
https://www.pexels.com/photo/9070966

Page 136: Wendy Wei
https://www.pexels.com/photo/1916821

Page 146: Cottonbro Studio
https://www.pexels.com/photo/7322300

Page 154: Andre Moura
https://www.pexels.com/photo/3839088

Page 162: Alexander Krivitskiy
https://www.pexels.com/photo/1098772

Page 162: Alexander Krivitskiy
https://www.pexels.com/photo/1098772

Page 168: Pixabay
https://www.pexels.com/photo/417070

Page 174: Thomas Mathew
https://www.pexels.com/photo/8293253

Page 180: Lucas Andreatta
https://www.pexels.com/photo/13347825

Page 190: Ave Calvar Martinez
https://www.pexels.com/photo/3839336

Ingram Content Group UK Ltd.
Milton Keynes UK
UKHW042048140323
418521UK00001B/112

9 781912 622399